RAVENWOOD
SPECIAL EDITION

AIRSHIP 27 PRODUCTIONS

Ravenwood Special Edition

An Airship 27 Production
www.airship27.com
www.airship27hangar.com

Agents of the Night © 2013 Aaron Smith (Reprinted from Ravenwood: Stepson of Mystery V2)
The Alchemists's Curse © 2013 Jonathan Fisher (Reprinted from Ravenwood: Stepson of Mystery V2)
Heart of Darkness © 2013 Gene Moyers (Reprinted from Ravenwood: Stepson of Mystery V2)
Jazzy © 2014 Ron Fortier (Reprinted from OCCULT Detectives V1)

Interior illustrations © 2013 Eric York and © 2014 Rob Davis
Cover illustration © 2016 Rob Davis

Editor: Ron Fortier
Associate Editor: John Bruening
Production and design by Rob Davis.
Marketing and promotion: Michael Vance

ISBN-10: 0-9977868-6-8
ISBN-13: 978-0-9977868-6-6

Printed in the United States of America

10 9 8 7 6 5 4 3 2 1

SPECIAL EDITION

Table of Contents

SPECIAL EDITION

"AGENTS OF THE NIGHT"

by Aaron Smith

The bushy-haired man shuffled slowly down the streets of Princeton, New Jersey. He was in no rush to get home, so he walked at a leisurely pace, paying little attention to his surroundings, his knowledge of the avenues automatically guiding his route as his mind, a mind of a capacity shared by few human beings of his or any other generation, wandered through time and space and the combination of both those ideas which is the universe in which we live. He walked along with the gentle evening breeze blowing through his once-dark, but now mostly gray hair, his briefcase hanging from his hand, swinging in rhythm with his gait.

He heard the footsteps approaching him, but he paid little attention to the sound; he often encountered other pedestrians as he walked home after classes had ended for the day. If those he met happened to be students of his or colleagues, they would nod in greeting but would not usually try to initiate conversation as they assumed, usually correctly, that the man they passed was thinking about something far more important than the mundane task of walking along the streets that surrounded the university.

The sound of the footsteps did not alarm him and so he was caught off guard. The shove was a hard one and the victim tumbled to the grown. He felt the hard, rough pavement scrape his cheek and he let out a small yelp of surprise and pain as the impact occurred. The world turned sideways as he lay there. One of his attackers kicked him in the side. The blow was enough to knock the wind out of him, keep him from trying to get up, but not hard enough that he felt or heard the breaking of any ribs. From his sideways view, he could see one of the attackers, a tall man whose face was obscured by the shadow cast by his fedora, force open the briefcase. The man's hand reached into the case, took something out, as the other hand made a gesture to the other assaulters. The man on the ground, the victim of the attack, thought he counted four of them, but he could not be certain. The briefcase fell to the ground with a thudding sound. The men who had come out of the darkness and struck disappeared back into the shadows and left the bushy-haired man alone on the concrete as he tried to pick himself up from where he lay. As the brutal strangers retreated from the scene of their crime, one of them spoke a single sentence.

"Enjoy the rest of your evening, Herr Einstein."

Thirty minutes later, Einstein reached his destination. He took out his key, opened his door, and calmly walked into his apartment. He dropped his briefcase on the floor and sat down on the couch, still pressing his handkerchief against his slightly bleeding face. He glanced around the empty apartment, still missing his wife, Elsa, who had died not long before. In one sense, Einstein was relieved that she was not there to see him arrive home in such a state, for she surely would have made a bigger fuss about it than was necessary.

To Einstein, the unexpected assault could have been much worse. All he had found missing upon inspecting the contents of his briefcase after his attackers had fled was a single notebook, one of several that he had been carrying with him. The notes inside that small book were not unique by any means. He had copies of them in his office at the university. He had lost nothing but a few minutes time and a few drops of blood. On the other hand, it would, he believed, be extremely unlikely that those who had stolen his notebook would have any chance of understanding or deciphering the formulae it contained. So while Einstein had lost nothing substantial, those who had attacked him had, he thought, gained nothing of any value to them. He wrote the incident off as a minor inconvenience and turned his mind back to the ideas that had occupied his thoughts before the sudden episode of violence.

"Ha! You have done exactly as I desired, Timothy! I am most pleased," said Desmond in the faux-English accent he often adopted when in one of his maniacally overconfident fits of glee. His dark eyes twitched as he opened the notebook and peered down at the numbers and symbols that were bunched together in the language of mathematics, the stuff of which science's understanding of the universe was made. Knowing that those particular equations had been written on those pages by the hand of the world famous Einstein, of all people, added to Desmond's confidence that the strange endeavor upon which he was about to embark, the weird plan that had prompted him to commission the theft of that very notebook, might truly prove successful and change the world forever.

Timothy, the man who had led the attack on the famous physicist, held out his hand toward Desmond. He expected his payment for the mugging and acquisition of the notebook. What he got was something else entirely. Desmond moved quickly and fluidly, and produced his pistol with great skill and speed. The sight of the long silencer on the end of the barrel had barely registered in Timothy's mind when the trigger was pulled and a single shot stopped his heart in an instant. The body fell to the floor. Desmond put the gun away, tucked the notebook under his arm like a schoolboy about to walk home after the bell had rung, and walked out of the apartment where Timothy's body would be found three days later when the old woman in the neighboring rooms complained of the foul smell coming through the wall.

Desmond drove his black sedan back to the small cabin he had rented in a secluded section of the Pine Barrens of Southern New Jersey. The Pine Barrens were, according to local lore, the stomping grounds of the legendary Jersey Devil. Desmond thought it quite appropriate, in a poetic sense, that it would be in that region where he would put Albert Einstein's equations to uses that the great scientist himself would never imagine they might be used for.

He got out of his car and went inside the small, log-walled structure. The cabin was empty. All that Desmond would need, he had brought along with him. He opened the bag he had carried from the car and took out the things he would need. He placed a candle on the floor and lit it with a cigarette lighter. It cast just enough light for Desmond to see the room around him and navigate in the space in which he was about to work. He reached into the bag again and took out a piece of chalk. With the chalk, he drew a large circle in the middle of the cabin, large enough for him to stand inside and maneuver around. He placed the candle just outside the circle so that when he was no longer alone within the circle, the entity that would join him there would not be able to snuff out that one source of light. The circle and candle in place, Desmond left the circle and stood to the side of the room where he stripped off his clothes and replaced them with a long black robe. He took out the notebook he had paid to have stolen from Albert Einstein and took it into the circle with him. As he used the chalk to copy Einstein's equations onto the section of the cabin floor that was within the circle, he thought about the chain of thoughts, what he considered to have been a true stroke of diabolical genius, which had brought him to that secluded location with those particular items.

Desmond had always known that there was more. He had felt it in his bones and in his skin and in the backs of his eyes and in the most intimate corners of his mind ever since he could remember. He knew…not thought or guessed, but knew…that what common men saw as the boundaries of experience were only flimsy illusions put up by our collective minds to keep us from glimpsing the awesome, awful truth and perceiving the true magnificence of the whole of the cosmos. There were things, Desmond was certain, far greater than any gods imagined by the Christians or the Jews or the Greeks or the Egyptians or any other civilization ever to come to prominence upon the earth.

Other men, some in recent times, Desmond realized, had caught glimpses of these ultimate truths and tried, however clumsily, to share these ideas with the world. The writer Lovecraft had certainly had some inkling of realization, but he had done no better than to hide his nightmares in popular fiction, placing hints within the pages of the cheap periodical, *Weird Tales*, but lacking the courage to shout the truth of the matter out for all the world to see and tremble at. There was also the English occultist, Crowley, who had, perhaps, uncovered some clues but who, like Lovecraft, had only had the resolve to go so far and write vaguely upon the subject.

Desmond had no desire to write of his recognition of worlds beyond worlds and the spaces between those worlds and the mind-blasting things which they contained. Desmond could never have been content to simply write of such things. He wanted more, he needed more, and he longed for more with every fiber of his being. He wished to experience those places and beings that were far outside the scope of mortal awareness. He would, he had sworn, change the world by uniting the inside and the outside, by opening the doorways that would allow the seas of infinity to spill into the small cup that was the known universe. Everything would change, and Desmond wanted nothing less than to be the catalyst of that change.

At first, he had thought he could bring about that change by seeking out the proper methods in ancient texts and long forgotten books of arcane lore. This had proved to be a dead end. For several years, Desmond had tried the traditional methods of occultism, but the end result was always the same: nothing. Then the answer occurred to him in a blinding flash of realization as he lay in bed one night in an insomniac's misery. The things he had been attempting belonged to the world of the past. How could he, a man of the fourth decade of the Twentieth century, truly believe in those ancient rites strongly enough to use them as a focus for his willpower and the force of mind needed to accomplish what he had set out to do? Indeed, he then understood that mankind's knowledge of the structure and nature of the universe had changed almost completely in the many centuries since the pantheistic religions had ruled the minds of men. In Desmond's time, even the monotheistic belief systems were not held in the same esteem as they once had been. It was science, or at least the unproven theories of the highest sciences, that captured the imagination far more than ancient tales of gods and titans. Why, he had thought, could the symbols and signs of that modern view of the universe not be used to bring the dark arts of sorcery into the present day? That, Desmond had guessed, would be the key to his success! And, he decided, if any man might be called the great magician or the high priest of that new religion of scientific speculation, it was surely the famous Einstein! Yes, Desmond had said to himself in his dark room on that sleepless night, if Einstein understands the cosmos better than any other man alive today, then it is his symbols that can be used, if I can use them properly, to open the door to the worlds beyond this small planet in this secluded corner of this pale and petty half-reality!

And so Desmond had hired men to go to Albert Einstein and take that small book which held the tools of the change which Desmond had sworn to bring about. Now, on a night that would seem, to most others, to be no different than any other night in the forested wilderness of the state of New Jersey, Desmond stood in that little cabin, all alone, preparing to complete the task that he truly felt he had been born to perform. On that night, he hoped and dreamed, his grand plan would come to fruition and the universe and the fate of the Earth would be forever altered.

Desmond stood within the circle. The floor around him was covered with the strange numbers and symbols of the equations he had copied from the stolen notebook. The light of the candle flickered and cast shadows upon the walls. Desmond gathered his willpower and focused his mind on the event he desired to cause. He looked up at the ceiling of the cabin, but did not see the beams of wood at all. He saw, instead, the stars above, shining in the blackness of the night sky. He visualized what he knew was really out there, choosing not to perceive with his physical eyes but with his vivid imagination. He imagined that he could see those distant stars up close and that his mind could journey beyond those faraway sources of light, travelling to the very edge of the small, limited universe in which his species dwelt.

He kept his mind focused on the vastness of what he knew existed beyond the boundaries of our universe. Once the idea was solid in his thoughts, he looked down at the floor, the chalky white sigils of his dark art, the numbers and indicative symbols of the language of mathematics shining up at him. Desmond did not understand what the equations signified, but it did not matter. It was the idea of their power, their hidden meanings, and their relation to the true nature of creation that would be the key to his opening of the great doors that kept the Outer Gods from entering our zone of life.

Desmond stared at those symbols for many moments until they began to blur together in his vision, a swirling, dizzy cascade of plus and minus and brackets and slashes and exponents and ones and threes and sevens and on and on and on until they became all that their watcher was aware of. Desmond could feel the sum of his universe and all other universes and all things that were not of any universe contained within that never-ending string of chalk strokes at his feet. The candle flashed, the room began to spin around Desmond, and he raised his head to the heavens and let out a cry unlike any he had ever released or even heard before, his vocal chords vibrating in a tone of unearthly power, a great call out into the depths of space, crying out, screaming out, begging the exterior cosmos to reveal itself to his small human mind, even if insanity or death should be the price of that knowledge.

The scream ended abruptly and Desmond fell to his knees, exhausted and numb from the intensity of the moment that had just passed. His eyes glazed with tiredness, he stared straight ahead at the wall in front of him, the light of the single candle bouncing its glow off the logs that made up that wall.

"Am I...am I still alone?" Desmond stuttered. He felt strange. The aura of the room had changed. He was not sure what had happened, but he could feel, instinctively on some level of perception that was usually dormant, that something was different after that experience and those flashing numbers and symbols, and that scream that had seemed to echo throughout all of time and space.

The voice that seemed to come from nowhere began as nothing more than a low murmur, a strange ringing in Desmond's ears. For moments it went on that way, just a buzzing. Gradually, it grew louder, more distinguishable, even comprehensible. It was rough, even harsh, but Desmond found that he could understand it. To his shock, he heard English being spoken, though he could not be certain if the voice truly did speak his language or if some sort of mind connection was instantaneously translating utterly alien syllables into recognizable words.

"The wall is...not broken! I can see you, small pale being of your primitive, fragile world! You can hear my words...but we cannot touch. Still...you have given me reach into your zone of reality, small though it is! From where I am...the place which only the darkest and mostly forgotten of your dreams have hinted at...I can exert influence on those in your world, puppets who will prepare the way for my true entrance!"

Desmond smiled in a twisted way. He was filled with the euphoria of sudden knowledge that his guesses and instincts had been proven accurate. "Yes, my...master! Tell me what I must do! I am your servant!"

"No, fool!" said the voice from beyond the universe. "You have opened the window, but you are too weak for my purposes. Yours is a mind of curiosity and dreams, but you lack the capacity for ruthlessness and the hunger for absolute power that I require in my servants! I thank you for your assistance, but your existence must now end, for you have seen too much."

Desmond felt a sudden pressure in the sides of his skull. He had no time to even hazard a guess at what was happening. The aneurysm burst as quickly as it had formed. Desmond fell forward and died before his face even struck the rough wooden floor of the small secluded cabin.

Spires of gold and other precious metals, decorated with gemstones and intricate carvings, stood high above the palace gates. Those front gates were guarded by soldiers with hats of fine fur and shields of solid steel, their swords hung at their sides in jeweled scabbards. The gates opened before the dreamer's eyes and the inside of the palace courtyard was revealed.

More armed guards stood inside the gates, all of them with the bearing of strong, skilled warriors, all of them bearing exotic weapons and wearing armor that shone like the sun in the afternoon. Servants scurried to and fro; running to fulfill their master's every wish. They were strong-shouldered men with loyal looks upon their faces and elegant young handmaidens in the splendid robes of Chinese courtesans, invitation written on their full red lips as they waltzed to their lord, ready to see to his every pleasure.

The eyes of the dreamer continued to look, searching deeper into the chambers of the grand palace, seeing priceless works of ancient art, shined and restored to brilliance, as if newly painted or carved, standing in their exhibition places in nearly every corner of the cavernous halls.

The twelve wives of the king danced along the corridor, each one as lovely as the prettiest of the maidens the dreamer had seen in the courtyard. Between the dancing wives ran the dozens of children, glowing with youthful health, the promise of bright tomorrows shining in their eyes, their cherubic faces full of smiles.

The dreamer saw the extravagant throne room, a long carpet of the finest silk leading to a small set of steps, atop which sat a golden throne. The king sat upon that throne and looked into the dreamer's eyes. The dreamer saw that he was the king, and he felt great pride and great power.

The palace and all the wonders within and around it were suddenly gone. The dreamer saw only darkness. It felt like many hours before the darkness and the silence were broken by a voice, but a voice did come, meeting the ears of the dreamer with a roar that would have echoed through the heavens had any sky been visible in the shadows of the dream.

"Did the palace and the kingdom and its countless pleasures make you desire them, dreaming man? They can be yours, I tell you. I promise you! I am soon to come into your world, dreamer on the small blue planet! If you will but assist me in preparing the world for my arrival, I shall reward you with all you have seen on this night of dreams! Would this please you, oh sleeping one? Will you help me to arrive?"

The dreamer did not hesitate. "I will," he said in his dream-words.

The voice said no more. The darkness and shadows remained for some time and then the dreamer awoke.

The man known as General Pao to both his friends and his enemies sat up in his bed. He smiled as he awoke, but it was not a smile of joy. It was a grin of pure greed. In his dream, he had been a king, rich beyond imagining, powerful as a god on Earth. His sleeping vision had given him a glimpse of something greater than anything he had ever possessed, and he wanted it.

His life in the San Francisco of 1938 was not an empty life by any means. In that city, he was one of the most powerful men alive, though few of what might be called San Francisco's average citizens knew his name. He was, however, feared and respected by the gang over whom he ruled and the people from whom he extorted money, took what he wanted, and had beaten or killed if they dared disobey him. He was also well known by the city's police, those men in blue and gold who sought his arrest or his destruction with increasing persistence. He was called General Pao. Though he held no official rank in any of the world's military organizations, he demanded to be addressed by that title. It was used as a sign of respect by his men and by those over whom he ruled in the shadowy parts of the city that possessed the famous Golden Gate Bridge.

General Pao, though powerful in his small corner of the underworld, was far from content. He could, in his best dreams, see himself as an emperor, a king, even a god. He had just returned to the waking world from such a dream. This dream had been different from the others, for there had been a new voice addressing him. He did not know where the voice had come from or to whom it had belonged, but he knew that his instincts told him to trust it, and General Pao was not a man who often doubted his instincts.

In Mobile, Alabama, Richard Baker awoke from a similar dream. He had not seen a palace, but he had seen wide open prairies of tall green

He smiled as he awoke, but it was not a smile of joy. It was a grin of pure greed.

grass with vast rising mountains far in the distance. A hot sun had blazed overhead and he had been able to feel its radiant kiss upon his dark brow as he had looked down upon many huts, some large and some small, that had been bunched together in settlements upon that great plain of grass. He had stood on a high platform and looked down from his perch to survey the lands and the people over which he ruled. In his hand he had held a great staff and on his head had been the high hat of a witch doctor king, seen as a god taken man's form by those who believed in his powers. In the dream, his magic had been strong and he had been raised to a position of honor by the people. The men of his land wished to be him. The women wished to lay with him and bear his children so that their offspring could be great god-men and possess the great magic like their father did. Not only men, but also the beasts of the jungle feared him and bowed down before him. The men of his own kind, of the tribes of his ancestors, would follow him into war or into peace, through the length of their lives or to the day of their death. The other men, the Europeans who had enslaved his people and taken their lands and sent them across the seas in chains would fear him and pray for death rather than face his mighty magic and deadly spear. All this had Richard Baker dreamed.

He awoke and stood up, his boss scolding him loudly, embarrassing him. "Damn it, Baker. How many times have I got to tell you, boy? No sleeping on breaks! I don't care if it's the night shift. No sleeping! You fall asleep and you never get back up in time! Damn it, boy; it wasn't too many years ago I'd have gotten away with havin' you whipped for doin' that. Now get back to work."

Richard Baker wanted to kill the man who spoke to him in such a tone, but he held his tongue and went back to the stove. He would have his vengeance soon enough. The voice in the dream had told him so.

"Richard Baker," the voice had said, "Help me to come into your world. Help me, and I shall give you back your name and your rightful place in your realm! Those who came before your father were no menial workers, no slaves of the white men! They were shamans and kings! Richard Baker is only what you are called here, in the land to which your ancestors were taken in bondage! You were born to be M'Baku! The magic of the golden plains is strong in you and I will allow you to reclaim it and take what you desire! Heed my words, M'Baku, and open the door to me…and I shall give you Africa!"

Mildred Glass woke up coughing. She squinted as the early morning light stung her eyes. She stretched her arthritic joints in agonizing distress. She reached for the cup on the nightstand, inserted her dentures into her mouth and then grabbed her spectacles and put them on, watching the details of the room grow clearer when viewed through the thick lenses.

An hour later, the old woman was at her breakfast table, the maid bringing her morning coffee. Mildred pretended to read the early edition of the *Times*, but was, in reality, paying little attention to the headlines. Her mind dwelled on the dream she had just experienced, a dream of an incredible intensity, a dream that had aroused an emotion she had not felt in many years. That emotion was hope.

Mildred Glass had never married, never had children. She hadn't wanted to. She had never been content to live the life that was expected of a woman in the place and time into which she had been born. She had never had any need to work, either, having inherited a generous fortune at an early age. While other women of her generation were marrying, giving birth, raising families, Mildred Glass had been a collector. She had purchased, over the many decades of her life, as many strange and obscure and, in some cases, frightening artifacts as she could find. She had, in her opulent manor, many weird objects of arcane origin. She had always hoped to find that one special piece of wood or metal or gem that truly possessed the power that myth or lore claimed that it did. She had, as far as she had been aware, always failed in that endeavor. So, at the age of eighty, Mildred Glass found herself isolated in her mansion, surrounded by display cases and locked trunks full of useless trinkets, petty baubles of great antiquity but no real power. Her possessions might have had monetary worth, but not a single one of them had been any help to her in scaring off advancing age, increasing weakness, or failing vision. No talisman or sigil had kept her teeth from dropping out of her gums or retained the color of her hair. Mildred Glass, despite her riches and the museum-like castle she inhabited, had turned into a bitter, lonely, hopeless old crone. She had expected to die before long, a faded skeleton of a once-beautiful woman, the remnant of a wasted life, alone except for the maid.

On that morning, though, Mildred Glass felt something else. A vision had come to her in the night. There had been words, too, a voice in that dream state. There was, so the faceless voice had claimed, one object among the thousands of esoteric treasures in the Glass Estate that truly did hold power undreamt of by man. What was more, the voice in the dream had instructed Mildred Glass on what to do with that particular object. Now, on this glorious morning, as she pretended to read the newspaper, Mildred Glass felt more alive than she had in several decades.

She swallowed the last of her coffee. She dismissed the maid, telling her to take the day off and leave the manor. She rose from the table and walked, slowly but surely, aided by a cane, back up the stairs. She did not return to her bedroom, but went past its door to the very end of the third story hallway. At the end of that corridor was a room, an attic space where no servant had ever gone, where no one, save for Mildred Glass, had been in all the years since she had inherited the house.

Mildred opened the door and walked into that room. She switched on the room's single light bulb and tried to remember which of the several dozen boxes would contain what she sought. She ignored the pain in her joints and the tired aches of an aged body and began to search, tearing the lids off the packing crates as if she had suddenly reacquired the vigor of a woman of a third of her years. She would not stop until she had found it.

❉ ❉ ❉

Casper Parker awoke to the sound of jingling keys. He sat up on the cot in his small cell, his wrists rubbing against the hand restraints that were always in place except for the three times a day when they were unlocked to allow him to eat. He looked up at the small round window that was high on the wall, too high to look out of, only there to allow some light to enter the cell. There was very little light penetrating the window at that time, an indication that it was still only early morning. Parker was dumbfounded. Who would be opening his cell door in the wee hours of the day?

The sound of the keys ceased and the door swung open. The guard was standing there in the doorway, a man called Jenkins, the guard who usually worked that shift. He stared in at Parker, but his eyes were strange. His gaze was unfocused, lazy, as if his mind was not aware of what he was seeing, as if he were in a daze.

"Stand up," Jenkins said robotically. Parker stood, feet firmly on the floor while his hands remained behind his back in their manacles. "Turn around," Jenkins ordered.

Parker turned. He could hear the several paces of Jenkins's boots as the guard approached. He could feel Jenkins's large hands coming into contact with his bound wrists. The jingling of the keys resumed and Parker felt the bonds released, his wrists were kissed by the air and he could move his fingers. He whirled around and confronted the man who had just freed him from his shackles.

"Why?" Parker asked, looking at Jenkins's glazed expression, emotionless and mesmerized.

"The voice," Jenkins admitted. "I am …a messenger. Leave here, Casper Parker. Return to the ways that led you here. You shall not be locked away again if you obey the words of the voice. The door is open to you now, Casper Parker. Go through the door and into the world so that you may help a greater one enter through a greater doorway! But first…you must kill me so that I cannot tell the others where you have gone. Do it! Do it now!"

Jenkins coughed once and looked at Parker, sense and reason coming back to his face. In an instant of awareness, he saw that Parker was with him and unbound. Fear came into the guard's face as he saw Parker's hands begin to rise.

The asylum inmate moved quickly and mercilessly, his fingers ripping into the flesh of Jenkins's face, tearing and rending. Blood splattered onto the walls of the little cell as the mutilated guard, slain almost instantly by a man practiced in the art of cold blooded murder, dropped to the floor.

Casper Parker bolted out the door, running down the halls as fast as he could move, careening past the guard at the front desk and bursting out the door and into the streets of Manhattan.

"Free, free, free, I am free!" Parker shouted as he ran through the shadowy streets. Lust for blood shone in his eyes. From the few words of the guard, Jenkins, before Parker had ended his life, Parker had understood what he had to do. The door would be opened for the one who spoke in the dream world. The door would be opened and he would come, but he needed a pathway.

"Roll out the red carpet!" Casper Parker cried out gleefully. "The red carpet will be made of blood!"

"Not now, not now, not now!" Ravenwood woke up screaming those words over and over again. He sat up in bed, his sheets soaked with sweat, his head throbbing as if he'd just pounded it against a solid brick wall a thousand times.

He rubbed his eyes and then his aching temples, slicking his sweat-soaked hair back and struggling to keep his balance as he got out of bed. He walked, slowly and tiredly, to his bedroom door, opened it, and called out down the hallway as loudly as he could while still struggling to catch his breath.

"Sterling! Coffee; I need coffee! Make it black and strong!"

A moment went by before the answer echoed back to Ravenwood's ears. "Yes, sir, right way, sir," said the British butler as he hurried out of his own room to make his way down the stairs to the kitchen on the lower level of his vast penthouse and do his master's bidding. He could hear the strain in young Ravenwood's voice and it worried him.

Ravenwood immediately felt a bit of guilt at waking his butler so abruptly and barking orders, but he knew that the dream he had just experienced had been no composition of his imagination, but a dreadful portent of something that even he, with all his knowledge of the hidden nature of the universe, might be no match for. The coffee would help, if just a little bit, to wake him up. He would have to come to full alertness as quickly as possible. Already, his mind was spinning as he wondered and hoped, uncertain of what to do or what to think. He knew what he had dreamed of, knew that he had caught, with his nocturnally wandering eyes, a glimpse of a horror greater than any the world had been faced with in many ages. The world, Ravenwood knew, was not prepared for what was, quite possibly, about to happen. He would wake himself and then he would consult with the Nameless One, the only being in the world in which he had absolute trust. Perhaps, Ravenwood thought, his mysterious and eccentric companion would be able to help him decide what to do.

Ravenwood stumbled into the bathroom. He would shave and shower and then head downstairs to consume his coffee. That morning routine, he feared, might be his last short period of normalcy until the impending crisis was either resolved or altered the state of the world forever.

Thirty minutes later, Ravenwood sat behind his desk in his study. He was surrounded by shelves containing hundreds of books, many of them rare volumes of esoteric lore. The window behind him let in the streaming morning sunlight in which floated the steam of his coffee. His head still ached from the stress of waking from his intense dream, but he was beginning to regain his focus, his thoughts were flowing quickly and clearly again. Despite his renewed clarity, worry was still his foremost emotions; not mere trivial worry, but heavy dread.

The Nameless One came shuffling in without knocking. The very, very old Tibetan mystic who had been Ravenwood's mentor and friend walked in slowly, as he always did, for he was beyond elderly in years...even Ravenwood could not have guessed the Nameless One's age...and stood before the desk, looking at his young friend with eyes that saw far more than what the accompanying mouth ever expressed in words.

"You are growing more and more perceptive with each passing year, my young friend," the old shaman said to Ravenwood. "I know that you heard it too...that voice from outside the boundaries of what we call our world...

and for you it sounded even nearer than it did to me. Now, boy, you are afraid, and that is as it should be. Were you not filled with fear at what this means, I would think you a very foolish young man indeed."

Ravenwood looked up at the Tibetan elder. "If it is truly attempting to come into this world, Nameless One, what do we do? This is no foe that can be fought with bullet or blade, and the magic of this plane, no matter how strong on Earth it is, cannot challenge one of the Outer Old Ones! I see little hope."

The Nameless One shook his head. Sadness was in his eyes, but that worry had not yet drowned out the possibility that a solution could be found. Ravenwood took note of that expression and felt, if only slightly, better. The ancient one spoke again.

"The hour of entrance is not yet at hand. Whatever event has brought it near…was not potent enough to truly tear open the doorway to admit the Old One to this realm. It cannot come in, but can only communicate. Surely it will instruct those whose minds are malleable and whose hearts are black and rotten, but they will have to do its work until the key is turned and the entrance gate released. We have time in which to plan a defense, but that time will grow very short very quickly."

Ravenwood listened to the aged shaman's words and then posed a question of his own. "I have to go back to the dream-state, don't I? I have to look for details."

The Nameless One nodded. "Yes, my young friend. You have the capacity to find what you seek…what we must learn if we are to have any hope at all of stopping a terrible change from coming to this small world. You must try. If you fail, all is doomed."

Casper Parker spent the day's hours running, ducking down alleys and side streets, concealing his presence from passersby and police. He could not afford to get caught, to be sent back to the madhouse. His opportunity had finally come; he had been called into the service of those from beyond. He would heed the summons, cause the blood to flow, construct a pathway on which the visitor who had spoken to him in the dream could walk and enter the world. When that arrival occurred, Parker knew that he would be among the chosen few to stand by his master's side and rule over the small, weak creatures that made up the bulk of the population of mankind. Parker vowed that he would not fail in his attempt to do what he knew he had to do.

He knew where he had to go. There was a woman he had to find. She would have a piece of the puzzle, a fragment of the key. It was no maiden he sought, nor a mother. He had to find the crone.

Several miles away, still sequestered in her attic, Mildred Glass tore the lid from the thirteenth box. She pushed aside the old, yellowed newspapers that protected the contents, and then she smiled a wide grin with her stained false teeth reflecting the light of the attic's single light bulb. She reached a withered hand into the box and took out a small smooth stone. She recalled buying it many years earlier from a desert nomad on the border between two Middle Eastern nations. She had paid only the equivalent of pennies for the thing, not knowing at the time what it was or what great significance it would someday have in her life. As she felt its strange touch for the first time in five decades, she suddenly understood what it was: a piece of another world, fallen to Earth from a now extinct planet that had once circled a now burnt out star, billions of miles away. She fondled that ancient stone like a part of a long-lost lover and she felt the warmth of the cosmic inferno caressing her greedy old heart.

Several states away from the Glass Estate, the man who had suddenly taken to calling himself M'Baku had just boarded a bus. It did not bother him that the laws of the state in which he happened to have been born forced him to sit in the rear of the bus. None of that mattered to him as the ride began. His past was over, he knew. Only his future stood before him now, and it was a future that promised him great power.

Across the country from the starting point of Richard Baker's bus ride, the man known to his friends and his enemies as General Pao stuffed a wad of cash into his trench coat pocket. It was the total take from the week's extortions. The money had been forced from the hands of the shopkeepers and merchants who paid to avoid pain, knowing that refusal would lead to the spilling of their blood at the hands of General Pao and his henchmen. Since those poor businessmen wished to avoid pain and possible death, they, with false glee in their voices, periodically handed over a percentage of their earnings to the Pao Gang. Now, the leader of that dreaded San Francisco crime clan would take that money with him to the airport and fly the nearly three-thousand miles to the East Coast. He would be guided not by a map, but by his instincts and the clues he had gleaned from a dream. He would go where the journey took him and, once there, he would meet others who had followed similar paths, and he would see that his dreams came true.

Ravenwood went for a long walk in the afternoon. He had spent the morning worrying about the events foreshadowed by what he had witnessed in his vision in the night. Feeling as though he were drowning in his concerns, he had chosen to get out of the stuffy confines of his rooms and wander the city streets, watching the people and reminding himself of why he had chosen to live his life as a man on the thin line that divided the light from the shadows, common perceptions from the secret knowledge of the stranger aspects of human existence, and the world as defined by science from the world of the supernatural, the occult, and the arcane. Ravenwood did, for the most part, enjoy the thrill of such a life of mystery and adventure, but he rarely faced such looming doom as he did on that day. He breathed deeply as he sat on the park bench that his walk had deposited him upon. He sat and watched the old men play chess, the children run at their play, the young lovers kiss under the sun-brightened willow tree, and the mangy stray cats try in vain to catch the mocking, taunting pigeons. He smiled at the scenes of normalcy and innocence, thanking the powers that govern the universe that most people lived life free of the burden of knowing too much about the great secrets of time and space and life and death. He vowed that he would do whatever was in his power to stop the terrible events that threatened to engulf the world in the flames of change and destruction and, potentially, tyranny from beyond the borders of creation.

He stood up from that park bench when he saw the sun beginning to dip towards dusk. He began the walk back to the penthouse. Once there, he would lock himself in his study and intentionally enter the realm of dreams and omens and astral visions. He would use his talents, skills shared by few others of his species, and travel the roads of space and time without the limitations of his physical body holding him down with its weight and density. He would learn what he needed to know and then use those hard-earned facts to choose his course of action. The survival of the human race and the good of the world had just become…and he truly hoped he would be up to the task…Ravenwood's responsibility.

When he reached home, Ravenwood told his butler, Sterling, to take the evening off. He wanted to be alone and meditate and seek information without there being any chance of interruptions, however minor they might be. The only other inhabitant of the penthouse, the Nameless One, would certainly know to steer clear of Ravenwood, especially when he was at work in the manner which the Nameless One had, after all, been the one to teach him.

Ravenwood went to his study and locked the door behind him. He closed the curtains; he would not need the kind of light that allowed his physical eyes to see, for he would not be using those eyes, but a different pair, an inner pair, in the use of which he was supremely skilled. He cleared the center of the room of all its furniture and sat down cross-legged on the floor, upon the circular crimson carpet that lay, perfectly centered, on the hardwood floor. He closed his eyes and began to control his breathing, slow and calm and steady and relaxed. The state he aimed for was a mixture of moods that could, to one uneducated in the ways of the arcane, seem contradictory. He needed to be perfectly relaxed, but also alert. His body had to reach the condition that hovered just between sleep and wakefulness, but his mind, once it began its strange, spying journey into the spaces between spaces, had to remain fully alert; in the astral plane, especially when one was investigating events as dire as that which Ravenwood was interested in, danger of the deadliest kind could wait around any corner or through any portal of dimensional transport.

Ravenwood, through a lifetime of honing his mystical skills, was able to slip easily into his astral avatar and fly free of the boundaries of the three simple dimensions we tend to perceive most of the time. He glanced down at his empty vessel, his body, and then was on his way, moving unconstrained by the laws of physics, moving not within time, but despite it; not within space, but regardless of it.

He entered the great realm where dreams are manufactured and he wondered where would be the logical place, according to the lines of logic that governed such a naturally illogical place, to begin his investigation.

He knew, with some certainty, what the great threat he had detected was. He knew that much, but did not know how such a great danger had come to loom so closely above the world which humanity inhabits. Knowing of the problem, but not what roots had sprouted it, Ravenwood decided to work backwards and begin with the identified problem and work towards discovering how it had begun. He knew where in the dreamscape he would have to go to accomplish such a thing.

He concentrated his mental energy, focusing his thoughts on the very edge of the vast dream world that he had entered. He willed his mind to let go of any intention that bound him to a particular place in the dreamscape and allowed his spirit body to be carried along on the currents that ran through space and time and dreams like mystical tides upon a vast sea of ideas.

He felt himself move, gently at first and then, abruptly and almost

He glanced down at his empty vessel, his body, and then was on his way,

alarmingly, at a great speed. He felt as if he were flying along at greater than the speed of sound, greater even than the velocity of light; he was, for he had allowed the universe to move him along at the speed of thought.

On and on he sped, so fast that his mind's eye could not register where he was, what was around him, or in what direction he was traveling. This motion went on for what seemed like a long time, hours even, but it was indefinite how much time had actually passed, for time that is measured by clocks in the waking world has very little meaning in dreams.

The stopping of the flight was as sudden and unnerving as the acceleration had been. Had Ravenwood been in his physical body and stopped moving so abruptly, the slamming of the metaphysical brakes would surely have torn him to pieces, but the dream body is not the physical body and can withstand such shocks, assuming that the traveler in dreams is skilled in such endeavors, as Ravenwood certainly was.

He had stopped and he began to look around. He saw nothing behind him but black emptiness, but before him he saw what could only be described as the far wall of the universe. Ravenwood knew that he had reached, in his mind's searching eye at least, the point where our universe ends and the outer realms begin. He, being a mortal being confined to this universe, despite his great power and skill in supernatural matters, could go no further, nor did he want to, for he knew that he would never be able to survive outside the universe, where the laws of physics do not apply as they do here. He could, however, since he knew of things that most men do not, see beyond the wall, through it, as if it were but a window between a house and the street upon which it had been built.

As he peered through that wall at the space beyond the familiar universe, Ravenwood understood that he did not see what was really out there, for his mind had built in safeguards to keep him from seeing too much, from seeing that which it would be impossible to understand, from seeing that which would lead to instant, irrevocable insanity. Men were simply not meant to understand that which dwells beyond, not even men like Ravenwood. That, the young mystic knew, was why he had to figure out exactly what was happening and how he could, if at all possible, end it before it went any further.

What he saw beyond the wall, or what his mind had translated the unspeakable horror beyond into, looked like nothing more than a great shadow, vast and dark and deep as any ocean, but still just a shadow. Yet Ravenwood knew that it was more than any normal shadow, for he felt things as he looked into that waiting darkness; he could feel a greed, a lust, a taunting and, most profoundly, a terrible unearthly hunger that he knew would only be satiated when the universe and all of its inhabitants had been consumed, in one sense or another, by the source of that shadow.

His greatest fears had been confirmed; Ravenwood turned away from the sight of the shadow, for he knew that it would be unwise to look into the darkness for too long. To do so would put his sanity at risk and he preferred not to gamble with his mind. He turned his attention to discovering how the shadow had come to loom so closely over the universe. Since he, a man of Earth, as opposed to a being in any other location in the space-time that made up our universe, had been the first, as far as he knew, to detect the coming of the shadow to the door of the universe, he knew that he could assume that the chain of events had begun on Earth. He focused his attention on the part of the dreamscape that represented his own planet and began to look up and down the lines of time to see if there had been an event of particular occult significance in recent days that might account for the shadow's approach.

As Ravenwood advanced his investigation, he kept in mind that he did not know exactly which shadow he had seen and what its precise nature was, though he was certain that it would destroy all that mankind knew should it enter the universe outside which it waited. There are many things in the beyond which are greater and more terrible than any god ever dreamt of by most men. Ravenwood knew that such a thing now watched his world and waited outside its door like a beast about to feed.

As he stared into the lines of time that represented the recent days in Earth's lifespan, Ravenwood saw a flash of arcane light, an indicator of something happening, of some meddling done by man to the state of the world's energies. He knew that had been the moment. He willed his mind to move close to that point in time and space, to try to glimpse, in more detail, what the scene of the meddling had been and what had been done.

He saw a face, a man he had never seen before. He saw insanity in the man's eyes, but also a deep willpower. He saw a flash of revelation and discovery cross the man's features as some new insight burst into the man's mind. He saw candlelight and symbols, symbols that he realized were numbers, mathematical figures, long strings of signs and numerals. After this, he saw a great explosion of smoke and fire. He interpreted this to mean that the man, the one with the numbers in his mind, had not survived his own experiment. When the dream-smoke cleared, Ravenwood could see the energy from the experiment flying from that place, wherever it had been, shooting off in various directions. Ravenwood knew what had happened. He was certain he understood. The ill-fated man with the numbers had half-succeeded in what he had been attempting, at the cost of his own life. The shadow from outside the universe had gained partial access to our world. Now it had fingers upon the Earth, tentacles of outer-world energy that would reach out and find servants and make them dance like puppets on long, ethereal strings. Those human puppets would manipulate further energies upon Earth and finish what had begun. They would open the door, the flood gate, and allow an Old One to enter the world. If that occurred, nothing would be safe.

Ravenwood had seen enough. He was beginning to feel weak, overwhelmed by the things he had learned. It would be wise, he told himself, to end the dream and rest, before the strain proved too great and he too became entangled in the webs of the terrible series of events that threatened to bring the gods of one realm into another. He returned himself to normal, waking consciousness. As his eyes opened and he saw his familiar study, lined with bookcases and smelling of exotic incense, he struggled to catch his breath, his mind racing with panic now that he knew his suspicions had been correct.

Ravenwood had been awake and back to his normal senses for only a few minutes when a knock came upon his study door, followed by the crisp British accent of Sterling, calling out to him. "Master Ravenwood, sir! Are you all right in there, sir? You've been shut in behind that door for so long, sir. Can I get you anything?"

Ravenwood stood up and stretched. His joints and muscles ached, making him wonder just how long he had actually been in the dreamscape. It was difficult to judge time in such a place. He walked over to the door and unlocked it, tugging it open to find his butler, worry on the servant's dignified face, waiting for him.

"Sterling," Ravenwood said, "how long was I…?"

"Nearly twenty-four hours, sir."

"A day…an entire day," Ravenwood muttered. "That…that thing outside the wall…it must have done something to the way I perceived time in there! If it could do that…that means it's grown stronger than I'd thought it had. This is all happening too fast! Sterling, I should eat. I know it's not exactly morning, but it feels like it is; bacon and eggs, please…and coffee, lots of it!"

"Yes, sir," the stalwart butler shuffled off to do his duty.

"Where are you?" Ravenwood said aloud when he was alone again. He was addressing, of course, the Nameless One. He knew that the ancient Tibetan could hear him no matter how many of the penthouse's large rooms and walls stood between the locations of their respective physical bodies. Ravenwood desperately needed to confer with the wise and aged man who had taught him so many things over the course of his life.

The voice of the Nameless One rang inside Ravenwood's head. When that happened, Ravenwood knew that his mentor was not able to come to him in his physical body, for he was out wandering the world in his spirit form.

"As you have been busy in the dreamscape, my friend," said the disembodied voice of the elder mystic, "I have been following a thread of darkness that weaves its way to a place not so far from where we dwell. An old woman, a collector of things, is host to a strange gathering. Men have come to her house; one by sneaking through the shadows, one by flying through the air, and one by the wheels on the road. With these four come together, the pieces are in place to forge the key that will open the door of doom! You must act now or the price will be most high and the world will pay it!"

The voice of the Nameless One stopped speaking. Ravenwood knew that the Tibetan had just told him all that he could. The rules of magic and mysticism were strange things and those involved in such matters had to play by certain metaphysical rules that often seemed to follow no strict logic. While the Nameless One was far older than Ravenwood and far more experienced in the ways of the occult, he was not often able to directly assist Ravenwood on his cases, apparently being limited by the exact nature of his own powers. Ravenwood did not fully understand precisely what the old mystic was, or was not, capable of, but he appreciated the sage advice and wise companionship of his mysterious friend and teacher.

Ravenwood thought of what the Nameless One had just told him. "An old woman, a collector of things..." the Nameless One had said. Ravenwood guessed immediately who the aged mystic had meant: Mildred Glass, a woman known to many among the occult community. She was old and very, very rich. Miss Glass had long been a collector of all sorts of antiquities, particularly those believed by their original possessors to hold some sort of magical properties. If anyone that Ravenwood knew of might have the type of object needed as part of a recipe to open the dreaded door to another universe, it would be Mildred Glass. Ravenwood knew where she lived. He also knew based on what the Nameless One had told him that she was gathering help, some sort of assortment of men who would assist her in her dark endeavor of finishing what the ill-fated experimenter had begun with his arcane use of the mathematical equations that Ravenwood had witnessed in symbolic form in the dream vision.

Ravenwood weighed his options. He could go straight to Mildred Glass's mansion and try to put a stop to whatever was going on there, but he feared he would find himself outnumbered and he could not afford to fail, for the fate of all the world was at stake. He needed to find help for he felt that it would be very foolish to try to go there alone. But who, he asked himself, could he rely on to assist him on such a delicate and potentially dangerous mission?

The man who now called himself M'Baku walked into the living room of the Glass Estate. He had changed his attire since his arrival at the opulent New York State mansion. He walked in dressed in the ceremonial headdress that Mildred Glass had given him. A large headpiece adorned with bones, feathers and talismans of African origin, and paired with a loincloth and two golden bracelets, M'Baku's new costume made him feel as if he were one of his ancestors, a mighty shaman on the plains of the land of his forefathers. He could feel strange and ancient power coursing through his mind and his body, his blood boiling with occult electricity.

His three companions looked up at him as he entered. The large Chinese man, General Pao sat puffing on a cigarette, his muscles bulging in his tan silk suit. The small, wiry man with the crazy eyes, Casper Parker, was busily rubbing two long daggers together, sharpening them. Mildred Glass sat sipping from a cup of tea. On the table in front of her was a small, smooth stone. While the stone may have looked quite mundane to the untrained eye, M'Baku could sense an alien energy radiating from the very old fragment of a no longer extant world from somewhere very far away. As M'Baku took his seat with his companions, Mildred Glass began to speak in her raspy, withered voice, a sound like dried corn husks crunching underfoot.

"Gentlemen…we are gathered here to end the age in which we have all been born and to bring about a new eon, an era of great mysteries and change. We four have what is needed to open the gates that divide this world from all other worlds. We have all been called by the one who waits for us to act. We must let him in! We must let him in!"

Casper Parker put down his knives. "Save the pretty speeches, lady. What do we have to do?"

"This," said Mildred Glass as she held up the small stone for all to see, "is to be the focal point of the energies that we must gather to open the great door. This is what we must do: we shall need magical energy and we shall need the substance of life as a sacrifice! Mister Parker, it will be your task to find blood! Go now and bring us two people. They must be young and healthy and you must take care that you do not bring the authorities to us in the process of bringing what we require. And Mister Parker, do not harm them needlessly. We shall need all of their blood intact when they arrive!"

Parker smiled. He was going to enjoy working for Mildred Glass. He stood up and ran out into the night. Mildred Glass turned her attention back to her two remaining companions.

"General Pao, you are here because you are intelligent, ruthless, and strong. You shall be charged with defending this place, our fortress of the dark arts, against any who might attempt to intrude and interrupt our work.

"And you, M'Baku, have been born with great potential for focusing the magical energies of this world. Such power has come down to you through many generations. When the star-stone is bathed in the water of life, you will be the one to take its great power and properly aim it to the edge of the universe, so that the dam may burst and the Old One may come into this world like a great flood of glory and change! Will you both accept these tasks?"

M'Baku and General Pao nodded. The shaman had a faraway, dreaming look in his eyes; he felt close to his history and to the souls of his mighty ancestors. The Chinese gangster smiled; he kept thinking of the palace he had seen in his dreams, and the throne upon which he so wanted to sit and command his kingdom, his concubines, and his conquests.

The Black Bat was not having a good night at all. It was his own fault; he had gotten sloppy and now he was in over his head. He had often warned himself against enjoying his nocturnal escapades to the point where he grew careless and now he had done just what he had so often tried to avoid.

In civilian life, the Black Bat was Tony Quinn, a young attorney who, as a district attorney, had been scarred and blinded when attacked by a vengeful criminal. A revolutionary operation, a cornea transplant, had restored his eyesight and more, endowing him with the ability to see in the darkest night. He had concealed his restored and enhanced vision from the public, allowing most people to continue to believe that he was blind. He now used his unique vision, combined with his blazing guns and his athletic abilities to confront crime on its own turf, going into the city's dark streets in a black costume, black cloak, and full face mask. He had become the Black Bat and spent his nights as the enemy of crime and the prey of the suspicious police of New York City.

That particular night had begun like any other for the Black Bat. He had gone out on patrol, parking his black sedan on a side street and taking to the rooftops, leaping from building to building looking for criminals to take out of action and victims to protect. Now though, he had found a world of trouble, for he had allowed himself to be spotted by a patrolman walking his beat and had failed to flee back into the shadows before the young officer could call for backup. Now the Black Bat was cornered on a rooftop, his grappling hook and climbing line dropped accidentally, his most avid pursuer, Detective Lieutenant McGrath and five of his men bearing down on him. The Black Bat was trapped by those who mistakenly considered him no better than the thieves and murderers he strove to apprehend or destroy. As much as the Black Bat wanted to escape capture and protect his identity, he knew he could do nothing that might injure the police, for the cops were only doing what they thought was their duty. The Black Bat would not raise his guns or strike out at those brave men who had cornered him. He was running out of options.

"Put your hands in the air where I can see them!" shouted McGrath. "I've got you this time, you stain on the face of this fine city! Surrender or I'll order my men to shoot!"

The Black Bat began to raise his hands, palms out and fingers spread to show that he was not reaching for his guns. The policemen began to advance, McGrath in the lead. The Black Bat's heart sank; Tony Quinn's double life was about to be revealed and, even if he somehow managed to avoid prison for the supposed crimes of the Black Bat, his reputation would be ruined, his law practice lost.

McGrath was ten paces from the Black Bat's position, his gun in hand, his men close behind him. A victorious smile had grown on his face, his personal mission to capture and unmask the Black Bat about to come to a triumphant conclusion.

Suddenly, as if from either out of nowhere or from the heavens themselves, a voice rang out, making the police, McGrath included, stop in their tracks and look around in stunned confusion.

"Stay where you are…all of you…and listen to what I command! You will not approach this black-clad figure; you will not harm this man…for I have need of him!"

The Black Bat stared at the police in amazement. McGrath and his men wore glazed expressions upon their faces. They stood swaying back and forth as if standing up while asleep, though their eyes were still open. The Black Bat himself felt unaffected by whatever strange occurrence had seemingly frozen the officers in place. "Is someone there?" the Bat said aloud. "Who just spoke? What have you done to those police?"

The Black Bat heard a slight rustling sound, a hint of movement to his left. He turned to see a figure stepping out of the shadows. It was a young man, in his twenties with black hair and in a dark suit. There was something familiar about the mysterious visitor, as if the Black Bat had seen him before but could not quite recall where or when, like the feeling one gets when seeing a character actor but being unable to recall what film they saw him in last. "Do I know you?" the Bat asked the newcomer.

"You may have heard of me," the stranger replied, "for I do have something of a reputation, though I try to keep my business out of the papers. Our friends, these brave policemen, will be fine, by the way. It was no difficulty for me to place them in a light state of hypnosis by a certain technique of the voice. In a few moments, they will come out of it and wonder how their prey, the Black Bat, has managed to elude them again!"

The Black Bat let his hands drop back down to his sides as he walked over to the black-haired young man who had come out of the shadows to keep him from being arrested. "Thanks for the assist. But you still haven't told me who you are!"

"The name is Ravenwood," said the timely arrival. "And it was no free favor I just did you. To tell you the truth, I am in need of some help that I think you may be able to provide."

"Ravenwood…" the Black Bat said, recognizing the name. "You're the occult detective I've read about in the papers a few times. I was never quite sure if you were some legitimate expert of the supernatural…or some charlatan with a habit of taking credit for the works the police really do. I'm still not convinced you have any real mystical talents, but that little trick you just did impressed me enough that I'm willing to hear you out. So what kind of help do you need from me tonight?"

"Can I assume you have a car nearby?" Ravenwood asked. "Or do you only travel by rope and rooftop?"

"This way," the Black Bat answered, gesturing for Ravenwood to follow him.

"Good," said the young mage as they made their way down a fire escape to street level. "I'll explain on the way."

General Pao walked out the front door of the Glass Estate as he heard a car approach. As he walked down the front steps, he saw that it was Mildred Glass's automobile, the one that Casper Parker had taken to go on his mission to gather what was needed to go through with their elderly hostess's planned ceremony. Pao walked up to the car, his tall, solid body casting a shadow in the path of the light created by the porch lamp. As he approached the car, the vehicle's door opened and Casper Parker got out. His hair was disheveled and he had a scratch, still slightly bleeding, down one side of his face. Despite his injury, he was smiling in a wild grin that actually sent a chill down General Pao's spine. Pao was no stranger to violence and brutality, but Parker seemed to enjoy the idea of mayhem a bit too much for the tastes of even a gangland boss like the large Chinese mobster from San Francisco.

"I caught 'em, General!" said Parker excitedly. "I was tempted to gut 'em right then and there and have my way with them after the fact…but I did as Old Millie said and didn't hurt 'em at all…'cept for a good hard slap when one of 'em got out of line and scratched my damn face up!"

"Well then where are they?" General Pao asked, peering into the car through the still open door and seeing no one.

Without verbally answering, Casper Parker walked around to the rear of the car and opened the trunk. Pao came up next to him and looked inside. Two young women were in the trunk, one had a large bruise under her left eye. Both had make-up smeared and ruined by tears, both were gasping for air as they clutched each other in terror. They were gagged. Pao reached in and lifted one out, carrying her into the house. As she looked up into his intense eyes, she fainted from even more fright than she had felt in the dark, closed trunk. As Pao carried her, he could hear Parker behind him, dragging the other girl by the wrist, muttering as his captive whimpered and begged to be set free.

An hour later, the parlor of the Glass Estate had been dramatically altered. It was now a scene like something out of some medieval black magic instructional grimoire. The curtains were drawn to allow no outside light at all to enter the room, not even the pale, soft glow of the moon. Only two electric lamps now lit the area. Mildred Glass had considered candles, a more traditional means of creating light in the near darkness that was used for dramatic effect in such rituals as the one they were about to enact, but she had decided against it. She was not sure what powers might be unleashed in that room and she did not wish to risk her precious mansion burning to the ground, taking all of her dear possessions with it, if some otherworldly force should upset the candles' footing and cause a fire.

In the center of the room, two tables had been pushed together to form a makeshift sacrificial altar. Upon that table, the two kidnapped young women were tied down. They had been stripped of the clothing they had been wearing when kidnapped and had been forced to dress in robes that Mildred Glass had purchased at an auction of ritual garments in a little-known catacomb under the sewers of Paris years earlier. Those robes were actually designed to be worn before a sacrificial rite, so the elderly collector of strange artifacts was quite happy to see them used for their proper purpose. Clad in only those thin robes, still gagged, and tied to the tables at the wrists, waists, and ankles, the two girls stared up at the shadows that danced on the ceiling, their eyes wide open with fear, their minds repeating, over and over and over, whatever prayers they knew.

Casper Parker sat in the corner, not speaking, staring lustfully at a ceremonial knife, old but still very sharp, once used by a Caribbean Voodoo cult, that Mildred Glass had given him for the purpose of the night's ritual.

M'Baku, still dressed in his African shaman's attire, sat on the opposite side of the room, mumbling to himself in a language that he had never, until his vivid dream, heard before. Already, he could feel the power that he had inherited rising in his body and his soul.

Mildred Glass stood, leaning on her cane, near the tables in the center of the room. She held the star-stone in her free hand, caressing its polished surface with her long withered fingers. Her dark, squinting eyes, thick spectacle lenses allowing her to see in the dim light of the grotesquely transformed room, were locked on the two frightened women, helpless and vulnerable in their bonds. Mildred looked at them there and recalled her own youth and thought of how, if the night's endeavor was a success, perhaps the Old God that was soon to enter the world would grant her a boon and restore her to the beauty she had possessed so many decades before, when her eyes were bright and her skin was soft and supple and her hair was a chestnut brown color instead of the sickly gray it had faded to in her old age. Perhaps, she thought, with the stone and the fresh blood and the power of the shaman's family line, she would see on that night, finally after so many years of seeking, the supernatural power that she had always believed in.

Outside the estate, General Pao paced back and forth in the darkness of the grounds, watching for anyone or anything that might pose a threat to what his companions were about to do inside the house. He listened to

The two girls stared up at the shadows that danced on the ceiling.

every sound the night made, waited for any sign of trouble. Periodically, his hand felt inside his jacket pocket as he reassured himself that his pistol was at the ready.

✳ ✳ ✳

"Are you serious?" the Black Bat asked, his voice tainted with heavy doubt as Ravenwood finished briefing him on the situation at the Glass Estate, the house outside the city to which they were driving at top speed in the Bat's black sedan.

"Look, friend," Ravenwood tried to convince his masked companion of the urgency of their mission in the night, "I don't blame you for thinking I'm telling you a big fish story. Let's make a deal. You can ignore all the really crazy sounding details if you want to. But even if you don't believe the more esoteric elements of the story, at least believe me when I say that there are certain to be crimes committed as part of what I suspect is happening at that crazy old lady's house!"

That got the Black Bat's full attention. "What kind of crimes?"

"Up to and including...murder!" Ravenwood told the night-stalking vigilante to whom he had gone for help out of desperation. "If they're doing what I think they're doing, it might involve some sort of sacrificial rite! If that's the case, some poor victim...or maybe more than one...is going to bleed for the mad cause that Mildred Glass and her companions have adopted. Please, Bat, I need your help. Innocent lives are at stake!"

"Sacrifice, huh?" the Black Bat sounded more and more concerned as he digested Ravenwood's words. "That's utterly inhuman! I'd find it hard to believe that there are still human beings, even in a country as supposedly civilized as this one, who would still engage in such practices...but I've seen too many horrible things done out of the lust for power to really doubt that there are such people. If any of what you've told me is true...I hope we get there on time!"

Ravenwood felt the car accelerate even more as the Black Bat's boot pressed down on the pedal. The young mystic was beginning to think he had made the right choice in calling on the Black Bat for assistance in his attempt to stop the mad quest that those in cooperation with Mildred Glass were about to embark on. On through the night they raced.

✳ ✳ ✳

Mildred Glass took one more look around the room and smiled. "M'Baku, come to me!"

The man who had, only a few days earlier, been a short order cook in Mobile, Alabama, rose from his chair and walked, tall and proud in his shaman's attire, to stand beside the wrinkled old woman who was about to help him achieve his destiny. No longer would he merely be Richard Baker. From that night on, he gloated in his own thoughts, the world would tremble at the name of M'Baku!

"Begin the gathering of the energy," Mildred Glass whispered in M'Baku's ear. The tall black man raised his arms in the air and began to chant out loud, his voice rising louder and louder, calling out to his ancestors and their vast, legendary power in a language that had never before been spoken anywhere other than on the African continent. As she listened to M'Baku's chant, Mildred Glass wondered if there was anyone else alive on Earth at that moment who had ever uttered, or even heard, those ancient sounds of magic and mystery.

General Pao, outside, could hear the chanting through the house's walls. As he stood guard on the porch, gazing out at the shadowy night, he could feel the energy in that deep voice from inside the Glass Estate. He felt the magic in the air and he grinned at the idea that his dream of power and conquest was soon to come true.

The headlights of the black sedan turned off like the eyes of a dragon closing as the car stopped, parked a quarter mile from the Glass Estate. Looking through the line of trees ahead, the keen night vision of the Black Bat penetrated the darkness and could see the house beyond the wooded patches between he and the building.

"There it is," he said, turning to his companion.

"You can see it?" Ravenwood sounded surprised.

"Sure," the Bat said. "Seeing in the dark isn't an issue for me. It's a long story, but there's good reason for that. No time for stories now though. We need to get to that house before anybody dies tonight! I don't have a flashlight for you. Sorry."

"There's no need to worry about my eyesight either," Ravenwood assured his friend. "There are ways to see that don't necessarily involve optics." With that revelation, Ravenwood started to move, making his way toward the house with the speed and agility of a well-honed athlete. The Black Bat, trained to physical near-perfection himself, followed just behind.

General Pao thought he heard something, a sound that was not part of the eerie cacophony that was coming from inside the house. It sounded to him…and his ears were quite sharp…as if it had come from the woods that surrounded the mansion. He pulled the gun from inside his jacket and ducked down behind the porch railing to avoid alerting any approaching foes of the presence of an armed guard.

The Black Bat and Ravenwood dropped down behind some hedges as they neared the front of the house. The Bat had seen movement on the porch, but the figure he had had in sight had abruptly vanished, probably hiding. Had their approach been detected?

"What do you see?" Ravenwood asked the Black Bat.

"There's someone there," the Bat told him, "and he's noticed us. He's concealed himself and he's waiting in ambush. That's no amateur guarding that house."

"Right," said Ravenwood. "We'll proceed with caution...but no gunshots from you yet. I don't want to alert whoever's inside that they have company. Do you hear that sound, that chanting? It's begun. We have to move quickly. How fast can you take care of that hiding guard without shooting?"

"Give me ten seconds!"

The gloved hand of the Black Bat felt around on the grassy ground. He picked up a stone and threw it with the accuracy of a Major League pitcher's fastball. The stone went flying through the air and struck a tree to the right of the Glass Estate's front porch.

Cued by the sound of the stone hitting oak, General Pao bolted up from his crouching position behind the porch railing and leapt, gun in hand, in the direction of the sound. "Who's there?" he shouted, loud enough to tell the Black Bat that his maneuver had worked, but not loud enough to be heard, over M'Baku's chanting, by those inside the house.

Ravenwood watched as the Black Bat went into action. The masked avenger did not hesitate. He sprang to his feet and ran, swiftly and ruthlessly, toward the Chinese mobster. Before General Pao had a chance to turn around and see the approaching mystery man, the Black Bat had launched himself the last few feet, closing the gap between him and his prey, and tackling Pao. The two men tumbled into a heap on the ground, wrestling for control.

As the two new enemies tussled, Ravenwood made a move of his own. He ran past the two struggling men and jumped up the three steps onto the house's porch. His hand met the doorknob and tried to turn it, but the door was locked from the inside.

Refusing to let a locked door stop him, Ravenwood let loose with a powerful kick. The door budged on the first shot, then cracked open on the second attempt. He walked in through the forced entrance and found himself in the front hallway of the manor. He began to follow the echoes of the strange chanting he had first heard from outside. Despite his training in the occult and his lifelong interest in the history of mystical cults, Ravenwood was uncertain what language the chanting was in, but he knew that it sounded very, very old.

The Black Bat had taken a hard punch in the face from General Pao, but shook off the stunned feeling almost instantly. He managed to narrowly avoid a second blow from the thick fist of the Chinese mobster. Pao's other hand struggled to maneuver his gun into the proper position to put a bullet right into the Black Bat's temple, but the Bat managed to knock that hand aside with a quick turn of his shoulder. The avoidance of being shot was followed by the Bat's gloved hand taking a slapped swipe at Pao's gun hand, knocking the pistol loose where it was swallowed up by the shadows on the ground. Pao's two hands, both empty now, reached up at the Bat's face, going for the eyes. This, unfortunately for Pao, left his face unguarded for a fraction of a second. It was just enough time for the Black Bat's next punch to connect, hard, with the Chinese man's face. The jawbone cracked, a tooth snapped, a thin line of blood tricked down the chin, and General Pao lost consciousness. The Black Bat pulled a length of rope from his belt. It was the rope he usually used to climb up the sides of buildings or rappel back down them. On this occasion, though, he used it to tie up the man he had just knocked out. He couldn't take the chance of Pao waking up and reentering the fight. The tying was done quickly and efficiently and the Black Bat stood and went to find Ravenwood.

Mildred Glass watched with amazement as the colors and light swirled around the head and hands of M'Baku. He was really doing it, Glass could see. The shaman was raising the energy, gathering the power that would be needed to charge the star-stone and use it to open the door that would let the Old One into the world. M'Baku's eyes were wide and star-filled. His body glowed with an otherworldly aura. His chanting went on and on. Mildred Glass took one last look at the star-stone as it had been since she had found it years earlier. She handed it to M'Baku and stood back.

M'Baku took the stone and smiled down at it. As he held it, his chanting lowered in volume to little more than a whisper. The eerie light of ancient magic continued to whirl and dance around his sweat-glistened body. The stone in his hand began to glow as intensely as the hand that held it.

"The star-stone must now drink of the fluid of earthly life so that the Old One will know the path it must take to arrive here with us!" Mildred Glass croaked out in her nasally dried husk scratch of a voice. "Casper Parker, rise and fulfill your murderous destiny! Let flow the river of crimson that will bring the Old One to us!"

The eyes of the two women on the tables began to overflow with tears. Both wished the horror they felt would cause them to pass out before the pain came, but no such mercy would find them. Casper Parker approached them, the long blade of his sacrificial dagger shining like the tooth of some mythical predator that stalked in the depths of humanity's collective nightmares. Parker stopped at the side of the first of the two women. He placed the blade against the girl's throat, his forearm muscles tensed and ready to draw the dagger across the delicate, soft flesh of the young neck.

"Stop!" Ravenwood shouted as he walked into the room and surveyed the scene. "This madness has gone far enough. In the name of all the spirits that watch over this world, I command you to cease this rite at once!"

"To Hell with you…you accursed interloper; this sacred ritual will go on!" Mildred Glass shrieked.

M'Baku handed the star-stone back to Mildred Glass and turned his attention in Ravenwood's direction. He raised his hands and bolts of energy shot forth, striking Ravenwood and sending him crashing into the wall.

As the African shaman attacked Ravenwood, Casper Parker, momentarily stopped by Ravenwood's intrusion, turned his attention back to the girl on the table. He put his blade back against her exposed throat, readying himself for another attempt at a merciless slicing motion. He never got the chance to make his move. A shot rang out. Parker felt a sudden fire in his shoulder. The dagger fell as his fingers opened. The knife clattered to the floor. Parker turned around, spinning just in time to see the Black Bat pull the trigger again. The shot was dead on. Casper Parker would never commit murder again. He had just faced his judge, jury and executioner, all clad in the same black cloak and mask, and the verdict had been 'guilty,' and the penalty 'death.'

Ravenwood struggled to his feet. He prepared himself for another blast of magical energy from the hands of M'Baku. When the lightning hit him again, pain surged through him, but he did not fall. He took a step toward the shaman who was attempting to kill him.

The Black Bat holstered his gun and went over to the tables in the center of the room. He stepped over the corpse of Casper Parker and picked up the dagger that the escaped killer had almost used on the two innocent women. The Bat used the dagger to sever the ropes that bound the two sobbing, hysterical young women. Both clad only in their thin robes, both trembling with fear, they were helped to their feet by their masked savior. The Black Bat unfastened his cloak from his shirt and wrapped it around the two shivering girls. He pushed them in the direction of the door, urging them to flee the terrible scene and make their way outside where they would be safer.

Ravenwood continued to try to advance toward M'Baku. The blasts of energy kept striking. Despite the agony caused by the arcane attack, Ravenwood managed to speak.

"I don't know who you are, Shaman, but I can tell one thing right away. You might be powerful…but you're an amateur! You're throwing all your power at me…but you have no skill, no finesse, and no sense of how to strike strategically and look for vulnerabilities in your opponent! A battle of magic is like a game of chess; it requires thought as much as it needs raw power. But you obviously haven't learned that lesson yet."

M'Baku howled out in his strange ancient language. His face told Ravenwood that he was getting angrier, growing frustrated that his magical attack was not felling his foe.

"I'll tell you one more thing," Ravenwood shouted over the sound of the energy bolts that still pelted him. "The problem with being a greedy, selfish dark sorcerer…which is clearly what you are…is that your kind generally doesn't have many friends to call upon in situations like this one. Those of us who value knowledge more than pure power have acquaintances on higher planes, and we know how to get a hold of them when we need to. I want you to meet one of my friends right now."

Ravenwood fell to his knees. He looked up at the ceiling, looked up as if he were looking through it to the stars. He had not fallen from the pain of M'Baku's attack, but because he had chosen to ignore the pain and focus on what he had to do to win the fight.

"I am Ravenwood, pupil of the Nameless One! I call out across the lands and seas of the Earth. I call out to the continent of Africa, a land of great secrets and powerful magic! There is one here, in this land far from your shores, who had stolen the ancient words of your magic, who has taken power that belonged to his ancestors but which he has not earned by the rites of passage that all shamans must pass through! Africa…I ask you to take back what is yours and to punish this usurper, this renegade son of your land! Take his power…and take him with it…and show him the way of the path he had not yet trod!"

The Black Bat, watching in amazement from across the room, was stunned to hear the sound of drums. At first, he thought it was thunder, but it was too rhythmic, too steady, and too eerie. He watched as Ravenwood struggled to stand. He watched as the bolts of fire stopped surging forth from M'Baku's hands. He watched as a strong wind blew into the room though no windows were open to admit it. He saw the wind knock the feathered headdress from M'Baku's head. He saw M'Baku begin to shake like a man freezing to death. And finally, astounded by the scene that unfolded before his eyes, the Black Bat watched as a brilliant flash of light exploded in the room and M'Baku vanished from sight.

Ravenwood took two steps forward and collapsed. The Black Bat caught him and helped him into a chair. "Easy, friend, you've exhausted yourself," the Black Bat gently said to Ravenwood.

"There's one more…" Ravenwood fought to get his words out before he passed out from the overexertion it had taken to vanquish M'Baku. "The old woman…where is she?"

The Black Bat looked around the room. "Over there! She didn't get far!"

The two men looked to the corner of the parlor. Mildred Glass lay sprawled on the floor. Her mouth was wide open, as were her glazed-over eyes. Her broken glasses were three feet from her gray head. On the floor in front of her, an inch from the reach of her outstretched, wrinkled, claw-like fingers was a small polished stone that she seemed to have been desperately trying to regain possession of when she had died.

"Heart attack maybe," the Black Bat muttered.

At the very edge of the universe in which humanity dwells, the Nameless One hovered at the wall that protects us from infinity. He watched as the shadow that could be seen through the translucency of the universal barrier moved slowly away, growing smaller and paler as the inestimable distance between it and us grew even vaster.

"You have done well, my young friend, my student, my son," the Nameless One said, though no other entity of any variety or species was close by to hear him.

"So what happened to the African guy?" the Black Bat asked Ravenwood. A week had passed. Both had recovered from the exhaustion and minor injuries they had sustained at the Glass Estate. They had met on the rooftop of the Sussex Towers, the building where Ravenwood's penthouse filled the topmost floor. "The old woman is dead and so is that Parker, the escaped maniac. The Chinese guy, General Pao they called him, is on his way back to California. I guess he'll go to Alcatraz. But the other one…he just disappeared in that little fireworks display you made happen! I don't really understand half of what happened there…but I just want to know one thing: is he dead? I mean…did you kill him?"

Ravenwood laughed. "No, I didn't kill him. I just sent him somewhere else. He was a natural at possessing some pretty powerful magic, but he needs to learn that there's a lot of responsibility that comes with such power. There are those in this universe who can teach him that lesson. He's with them now. Eventually, he'll make a choice. He can use that power like he tried to last week, for greed and power and personal gain...or he can use it for good. I hope he chooses the latter...and I hope I run into him again someday, as a friend next time."

"Hmm," the Black Bat said no more on the subject. He tossed his hooked line onto the roof of the adjacent building, pulling back on it to make certain it had caught. He swung off the roof to the next one, disappearing into the shadows without looking back. He had had enough of magic and mumbo-jumbo for a while. He wanted to get back to the basics: bullets, fists, and justice.

Ravenwood watched the Black Bat vanish into the rooftop shadows. He was glad to know that he had an ally, however skeptical, out there among the shadows. He suspected it would not be the last time he would find himself working with the Black Bat.

The End

MIXING AND MATCHING

Crossovers! Growing up as a comic book fan, I came to love crossovers and guest appearances. What fan wouldn't love series like *Marvel Team-up* or *The Brave and the Bold* where we got to see Spider-Man or Batman in some crazy situation where they would have no choice but to join forces with another hero to face whatever the great threat of the month happened to be?

Getting used to seeing crossovers like that, I couldn't help imaging what combination of characters could happen in other media, like movies or television, were such things not prevented by different networks or studios. What if Lieutenant Columbo took a vacation in Honolulu and had to help Steve McGarrett solve a murder? What if Captain Kirk and the crew of the Enterprise found a derelict spaceship containing suspended animation chambers and opened up one of those pods to find Captain America inside in his tattered costume and still clutching his legendary shield? Would James T. Kirk recognize Cap from his history books? Would Spock raise an eyebrow at the sight of the star-spangled, red, white and blue costume? Would McCoy blurt out a variation of his famous catch phrase, "He's not dead, Jim?" What if little Kal-El's pod had landed deep in the jungles of Africa and he'd been raised by Tarzan? Would we have a Superman of the jungle?

Those stories will, unfortunately, never be written. But we can imagine them!

One of the great joys of writing characters that are now in the public domain is that combinations and crossovers are fair game, and I love it! In my first novel, *Season of Madness*, I combined the worlds of Sherlock Holmes and Dracula by having Dr. John Watson team up with Dr. John Seward. In my Hound-Dog Harker series of stories, I've had Harker, himself a continuation of a character hinted at in *Dracula*, cross over with the worlds of Jules Verne's work, the stories of H.G. Wells, and also with Sherlock Holmes. Why stop there?

That brings me to the story in this book. "Agents of the Night" is my first story to feature the character of Ravenwood, but my third to include the Black Bat. Ravenwood is new to me, but the Black Bat, after two previous stories, feels like an old friend. I think they go well together. Both are creatures of the night, though in very different ways. Working on this story, it sort of felt like doing a crossover, with differences and in an earlier time period, between two of my favorite comic book heroes, Dr. Strange and Batman. Or Dr. Strange and Daredevil, I suppose, since the Black Bat shares certain characteristics with both the Caped Crusader and the Man Without Fear.

I'm happy to be able to do such crossovers with these amazing old pulp characters and I'd like to thank their creators. Also, since I never would have developed an interest in the pulps without being exposed to the comics that came later, I should also express my gratitude to those who created and those who introduced me to the aforementioned Dr. Strange, Batman, and Daredevil. So here's to Stan Lee, Steve Ditko, Gene Colan, Frank Miller, Bob Kane, Bill Finger, Dennis O'Neill, Jim Aparo and so many others who worked their creative magic on those classic characters!

AARON SMITH - is the author of 26 published stories, many of them for Airship 27 Productions. His pulp work includes stories in both volumes of Black Bat Mystery, four Sherlock Holmes stories, the Dr. Watson novel *Season of Madness*, and stories featuring Ki-Gor, Dan Fowler, and his own creations, Hound-Dog Harker and the Red Veil. His latest novel is *100,000 Midnights* from Musa Publishing. Information about his work can be found on his blog at www.godsandgalaxies.blogspot.com

RAVENWOOD
SPECIAL EDITION

"THE CURSE OF THE ALCHEMIST"

by Jonathan Fisher

Ravenwood hefted the intricately carved walking stick, and used the pommel to ease the library door open. It creaked painfully, just like the rest of the old house on 817 West Hampden Street. The whole neighborhood was broken, disgusting. The few residents who remained looked angry, downtrodden, like they'd cut off one's fingers just for the ring on it.

Ravenwood was familiar with such things, and it didn't trouble him. All that time studying eastern mysticism had taught him how to quiet his mind and his fears. All that being said, the old house still made the hair on the back of Ravenwood's neck stand on end.

The door swung open far enough for him to see inside the library. The walls were covered in an unorganized mess of books and specimens contained in jars of varying sizes. He squinted at the jars, and realized they were full of creatures, most dead, some still crawling or slithering around inside. Others had eyes, ears tongues, and other small pieces of the human anatomy.

"Mr. Ravenwood," a terrible old voice creaked. "It is good of you to come."

"It was you who woke me?" he asked skeptically. He doubted this old bag of bones could lift a feather, let alone a phone. She turned her withered face to him and glared.

He lowered his gaze and said, "What can I do for you, madam?"

"Do you know what this is?" she gestured broadly to the library.

"It reminds me vaguely of a collection of curiosities," he said. "They're called natural history museums now."

Again she glared at him. He met her gaze. If there was enough light for her to see the color of his eyes, she'd see it go from green to a dark gray, showing his mood of indifference. "What do you want?" he asked again, this time with more force.

"You are impatient, and I don't like it."

"Very well," he said, and hitched his walking stick up, "I bid you a good morning, madam." And he turned sharply. He was pulling the door open to step through it when a knife flew past his head and buried itself in the door-jamb, exactly at neck level. Adrenaline flooded his body as the surprise washed over him in a brutal wave.

He wheeled around, custom-built Luger automatic in his empty hand, and pointed it at the old woman. She had another dagger in hand, "It'd be well worth your time to listen to me."

"You've got my attention."

She smiled and it made his skin crawl, "Good. Come over here." She lowered the dagger. "And bring the knife."

He stuffed the pistol back into the holster under his left shoulder, and wrenched the knife out of the wall. It was balanced perfectly, and in haft was a carved pentagram. He looked at it curiously as he handed it back to her and asked, "What's this all about?"

"A theft," she said angrily, "Three days ago, my most prized research journal was taken. I called the police, but they tell me that they have no evidence of a crime, and therefore cannot search for it."

"Do you have any idea who'd want to take it?" Ravenwood asked as he looked around the shelves. It was an intriguing collection of macabre things. There were books stacked between the vases of creatures, some of them with symbols on their spines denoting the religion or cult they represented.

"Of course I know who took it," she snapped angrily, "It was my late husband."

"You're saying a ghost took your journal?"

She nodded hard. "I know it."

He took a deep breath and tapped the walking stick down hard, "What would you have me do?"

"Find the journal. My husband was resting peacefully, and someone changed that. Made him malevolent. I want you to find the journal and help me put him at peace once more."

She picked up a small beaker of a white crystalline substance, "Salt, to protect yourself in case he appears again. Draw a circle of it, and he can't pass."

He took the canister and slid it into a pocket of his coat. She hesitated, as if she had more to say, then she turned and said, "If he's been brought back, he'll probably be angry. Maybe even dangerous."

Ravenwood nodded slowly, but he was skeptical. So many times what seemed paranormal, even supernatural, turned out to be grounded in reality in some way. But he'd humor her.

"Yes, ma'am, I will be careful."

"Thank you. And do hurry, Mr. Ravenwood. The longer he's not at rest, the greater the odds that he'll be trapped here forever."

"Absolutely." He smiled and hitched up his walking stick. "Then I haven't a moment to lose."

She shook her head, and stood out of his way. He left quickly. Out on the pock-marked street, he climbed into his 1936 Ford H-Body with a well-tuned engine. He fired it up and pulled away from the curb in a flurry of tire-smoke and screeching tires. If he had to be up at four in the A.M., he wasn't going to be alone.

While he drove aimlessly back towards his penthouse, something gnawed at him. Cruising in fourth gear up Broadway, he tapped the pommel of the walking stick absently. He could see people on the streets as the working underbelly of the city woke up. They were tossing newspapers down, opening up shops, bringing in morning shipments, getting ready for the daily grind. When he stopped at a red light on 32nd and Broadway, he looked to the curb.

In his mind's eye, he saw the small newsstand attendant glance up and admire the car. Two seconds later, it happened. Ravenwood smiled, and nodded at the young man. He waved. The light changed, and he pulled away slowly.

That happened whenever Ravenwood focused on the world around him specifically. He could predict what people would do, what would happen when he entered a room. The entire time he'd been in the old woman's house—he could predict nothing.

A quiet voice wafted through his mind, "You'd do well to be wary of that woman."

It was the voice of the Nameless One, his mentor from the remote province of India where he'd learned the skills of foresight and the hunting of things paranormal and supernatural. When Ravenwood returned to the America and his home in the penthouse suite of the Sussex Tower, the Nameless One came with him, never to leave the room Ravenwood provided him with.

"I will be," Ravenwood said quietly, as not to draw attention to himself. "What do you make of her?"

"She tells you not the whole truth," he said, "But there is something evil lurking."

Ravenwood nodded, and angled onto the one-way access road back to his penthouse. The voice of the Nameless One was an eternal one, both incredibly aged and ageless at the same time. He appeared first to Ravenwood while in the little village of Brumah near the forbidden Tibet. Ravenwood and his father were standing watch for tigers, when the aged and ageless voice said, "Tiger!" and the elder Ravenwood had been able to fell the beast before it killed the Nameless One. In his native tongue, the old man had said, "Always the Nameless One will guard you and your flesh!"

When Ravenwood's parents died, the old man kept his promise, and had not left the young man since.

Ravenwood knew that his counsel would be valuable in this case.

※ ※ ※

Ravenwood angled the sleek, black Ford into the underground entrance of the Sussex Towers, and climbed out. He donned his expensive fedora and handed the keys to the valet parking attendant. Just inside the gold-plated double doors was a tired looking police chief named Inspector Stagg. He had deeply set eyes, was short and stocky. He had a small bag of peanuts in his right hand and was methodically transferring them to his mouth to munch on.

"Inspector," Ravenwood said kindly, "What can I do for you?"

"You can go bury your head," he said, "But since you won't do that—you can look at something for me."

"What kind of something?"

The inspector hauled a rolled-up manila envelope from the inner pocket of his overcoat and shoved it towards Ravenwood. The contents turned out to be a picture of an overturned gravestone with a dug-up grave in front of it.

"Why is this the business of an inspector of homicide?"

"Because the person buried there was murdered, two years ago."

"Did you close the case?"

Inspector Stagg snatched the photos away from him, "Did I close the case," he said sarcastically, "You never cease to amaze me."

"What do you want from me, Horatio?" Ravenwood cast the inspector a side-long glance as he said his proper name, which drew an angry stare from Stagg. The younger man laughed quietly to himself.

"I want you to go over to the cemetery and just look around. Don't ask any questions, don't dig too deep. I'm doing this for the family. They've been through enough without having their daughter's grave desecrated."

"I'll be discreet. Is there anything I'm looking for in particular?"

"I'm asking you to do this, so when I call them tomorrow morning I can tell them honestly that I did everything in my power to see that this unfortunate incident has been thoroughly investigated."

"And if I find anything out of the ordinary?"

"I don't wanna know. It's yours to do with what you will. I've got bigger fish to fry right now."

"I'm sure the family doesn't think so," Ravenwood said.

"You let me do my job, and stay out of my way," he sighed, and popped another peanut into his mouth. "I may think what you do is just smoke and mirrors, but if having you on the job makes the family more comfortable, then I'll bite that particular bullet."

"That's very decent of you."

"Don't let it get around." Stagg walked away.

"Last question," Ravenwood said. "Can you use your information bureau to tell me where Ivan Korduski was buried?"

Stagg hesitated, then nodded, and walked to the phone on the wall in the lobby of the building. He dialed the Research and Information Bureau of the NYPD, and relayed the information. A minute later, he came back and said, "It seems your man is buried in the Chapel Hill Cemetery, on 41st and Dumont." He tossed two more peanuts into his mouth and said with a sideways glance, "The exact same cemetery where the grave of the girl is located."

Ravenwood shrugged, "It seems we're destined to work together after all, Inspector."

"Uh-huh," the older detective said tiredly. He left, shuffling through the door silently. Ravenwood decided against returning to his apartment, as he had all the basics he'd need for looking over the graveyard either on his person or in the trunk of his Ford.

He went over to the doorman and valet attendant and smiled. "I'll need the car again."

The young man nodded, and walked off to retrieve it. Two minutes later, he was back on the road, winding through Central Park to the cemetery on the farthest side, between a couple of old gothic revival tenant buildings.

There were two NYPD Fords sitting out in front of the crooked wrought-iron gates. The cops looked all manner of anxious. He climbed out of the convertible and donned his black fedora with the red silk band around the crown, and approached.

"Morning fellas," he said, "How goes it?"

Neither of them answered, only stood up a little straighter. Ravenwood smiled as he passed them, "I won't be long, I promise." Still neither man spoke. He turned his attention to the cemetery before him.

Most people are naturally nervous around cemeteries. They are afraid of things they don't understand. If it doesn't fit into the nice little bubble that is their world, they want no part of it. It was a shame, as far as Ravenwood could fathom, because so much of the world is explainable if one is open to things that aren't openly proven, supposedly, through science.

He tapped his walking stick absently on the moist ground. He pushed back his fedora as he approached the first scene. At the yellow wooden police barricades, he hesitated long enough to shrug out of his coat. He knelt by the edge of the plot.

Heaped to one side was an expansive pile of dirt. The coffin beneath was barely visible because of what kept slipping back in, either from elapsed time and wind, and the police milling about. Their abilities to disturb a crime scene to destruction were quite formidable indeed. At least here, Ravenwood noted, the scene in the ground seemed to be more or less intact.

He looked around quickly, saw no one looking his way, so he slid over the edge, and dropped on top of the coffin. His shoes hit with a dull thump that echoed inside the coffin.

"Okay," he said, "Weird part number one." He tapped the base of the walking stick against the coffin and said, "Why is there an empty coffin in this plot?"

With his left hand, he began brushing off the dirt on top of the casket. As he did, he noticed that whoever had dug into this particular grave had dug favoring the right side. He looked it over, and at first could spot nothing out of the ordinary.

"Look deeper," the aged and ageless voice of the Nameless One said quietly. Ravenwood shifted carefully and with the end of the stick shifted the dirt around. A moment later, the end of the staff scraped against rock. Ravenwood reached down and moved some of the dirt by hand.

"A stone floor?" he wondered aloud. That's certainly what it appeared to be. An idea sparked in his mind and he immediately climbed off the casket and moved to the right. He found the small lip on the edge of the casket, and hefted. He strained mightily, but he couldn't make it budge.

He worked the stick around, and then twisted his entire upper body to put the most force he could muster into the hit, and smashed the stick against the side of the casket. The wood creaked, and he heard a shout, but he kept working.

He hefted at the lid of the casket again, and again it resisted him, but for only a moment. It gave way suddenly and lurched open.

"You can't do that!" the policemen yelled. He looked up and saw them holding their guns at him.

"Tell me, gents," he said seriously, "can you defile an empty coffin?"

"What?" the older detective said suddenly, "What do you mean?"

"Look for yourself, boys," he said seriously, and stood back for them to see inside the casket. It was lined with silk, but there were only round weights on the bottom of the casket.

Immediately, the older detective began crossing himself and backing away from the hole. Ravenwood said, "I don't think that's all, either."

The coffin was empty—no decaying body, no stench of something rotted. In fact, it looked like it was brand new, on the inside at least.

"When Inspector Stagg gets here, you can tell him where to find me." Ravenwood sat down on the edge of the casket and began running his hands over the lining. A moment later, he found a small metal switch, hidden within the folds of the white silk. He pulled it, and the bottom of the casket dropped straight down, and the lid slammed closed.

Ravenwood recoiled hard away from the casket just as the lid banged shut. His walking stick was inside the casket, and he swore quietly. His suit was now soiled with wet dirt. He shook his head slowly, and then levered the casket open again.

"That explains why this was so hard the first time," he muttered. When it was open again, he rolled inside. The casket was cramped, as it was clearly not built for his tall, athletic build. He found the lever again, and the bottom dropped out as the lid of the coffin slammed closed.

He fell straight back, as soon as his arms were free of the confines of the coffin he stretched out. He landed hard, flat on his shoulders and upper back, on a padded surface that shoved him onto a slope. His whole body shifted in a slow circle as he picked up speed in his slide. He saw lights down at the end of the slope and he tried to brace himself, slow down somehow.

Nothing worked as he careened into the light. He hauled his Luger out as he hit the bottom hard, and the wind was knocked out of him. Blackness clouded the edges of his vision. He took a couple of deep breaths and gagged on the dust.

He stood up slowly, the Luger in hand, and looked around. The passage he was standing in was narrow, made of stone, and covered in dust. Most of the floor had a thin layer of dirt over it.

He brushed himself off as best as he could, and noticed the walking stick had rolled almost a dozen feet from the end of the slope. He picked it up, and started down the tunnel.

The sense of claustrophobia inside the tunnel was starting to wear on Ravenwood. Lit torches were spread out every twenty feet or so with wide patches of darkness between them. He saw spiders skitter out of sight whenever he stepped into the light again. Despite knowing that he'd see it coming, he kept looking over his shoulder, uncertain he wasn't being followed.

He moved through the narrow labyrinth until he rounded a corner and saw a wide, short room that he could only just stand up in. There was a wooden table with metal legs in the center, and red candles were spread throughout on six-armed candelabras. Before he walked very far into the room, he stopped at the entrance and laid out a line of salt. It'd stop any malevolent entity from coming in, and create a line that he could escape across if anything attacked him. With that done, he looked to the room.

"What goes on here?" he wondered aloud. The table was a dark wood, and stained in the middle with an ugly varnish. He adjusted his fedora, and looked around the rest of the room. It looked like an old crypt, which had been converted; where bodies used to lie after they passed now books were stored. Candles made the room clearly bright which contrasted with the feeling of ill-will that hung over the whole room. It was a choking sensation, painful in its intensity.

He began tapping his stick anxiously, trying to get a read on the room. It took him a long moment to realize that the only thing he could sense was the agony that had been experienced in this room.

He realized that the dark varnish on the table was blood. Cold fingers danced up his spine and made him shudder. He put his back to the table, and looked at the books instead. Several had upside down pentagrams on their spines, denoting them to be of a specific segment of the occult. The baby-killing kind.

Ravenwood dearly hoped that he didn't have to deal with that kind of fanatic this time around. He ran one gloved finger over the spines of the books, taking time to remember their names to trace their origin. These were rare volumes—if he could find the supplier, he could find the...

A rock scuttled in the hallway. He twisted around, Luger raised, and pointed the hand-gun into the corridor. Nothing moved at first, but gradually Ravenwood noticed that the torches were wavering like something had just run past them. He tightened his grip on the pistol and approached the entrance to the small sacrificial chamber slowly.

He heard a gust of wind behind him and twisted around. He fired off a shot at the rushing object but didn't slow it down. A terrible shriek echoed brutally, stung his ears, and sent him staggering backwards as the beast roared past, cutting through the fabric of his left sleeve and gouging his arm.

The candles and torches went out with a whoosh, and a clinging darkness fell over the entire room. He swallowed hard, then adjusted his grip on the walking stick. He backed up against the wall, and began muttering quietly in Sanskrit—the language the Monks who'd carved the unique stick taught him.

A light flared on the bottom of the stick, but it didn't do as much good as he'd hoped. He tapped some of the mud off, and an eerie blue light swept through the chamber.

"You are not alone," the Nameless One said quietly. "But I know not what haunts you now."

"Great," he retorted. He held the walking stick up, and aimed the Luger in the same direction as the light. He was no wizard, and summoning the illumination wasn't a magic trick—the process was simply transformation—taking one source of energy and turning it into another one. It's simply accomplished through intense focus brought about by reciting a very intense and complicated phrase.

Ravenwood stepped into the hallway and swept the light, and his gun, back and forth. He saw no presence of what had blown the lights out and had attacked him. He turned around and cast one last glance around the room.

"Am I missing something?" he asked the Nameless One.

"You'll know it when you see it."

Quickly, Ravenwood walked back into the room, the Luger down by his side. He looked at the floor, kicked the books that had fallen around to look for other objects, and had nearly made an entire circuit of the room when he spotted it. As he stared at it, he thought it'd be hard to miss, despite the fact he did so at least twice.

It was a journal—identical in the way it was manufactured, right down to the same seven-pointed symbol on the cover of the leather to the journal the crazy old woman had given him.

"Strange," he decided. "Very strange indeed."

He left the sacrificial chamber, and started down the corridor to the right. It led up to another, gentler slope. He was able to climb this one, and at the top of the incline he found a thicker and broader landing cushion. He looked up through the narrow opening, and saw the bottom to another coffin. He stood up carefully in the opening, and found the edge. He pulled it back, and stood up inside the casket. He pushed against the lid, but it refused to budge.

"Bollocks," he said tiredly. "Now what?'

"How would he that does the ceremonies of blood leave?" the Nameless One asked.

Ravenwood slid down the incline, and kept walking down the tunnel. A moment later, he came to a corner, rounded it, and found himself at a heavy wooden door. He tried the knob, found it locked. He groaned quietly, then hoisted his Luger, put the barrel in the key-hole, and squeezed the trigger.

The shot was deafening in the confines of the tunnel, but when he tried the knob next, it opened after a little bit of jiggling. He shoved through the door, and found himself in the basement of the mortuary building on the cemetery grounds.

When he left, he saw almost a dozen policemen around the grave of the young girl who was not actually buried. He tapped out the light from the walking stick, stowed the Luger, and approached the cops.

"Gentleman!" he called, "I don't think you'll find me by staring into the hole."

Most of the cops wheeled with surprise and shock at his sudden appearance. Inspector Stagg looked up angrily. Ravenwood approached, and smiled. He said, "This has become most peculiar, Inspector. If it's no trouble, I'll be looking into it further."

"And where would you start?"

Ravenwood pondered that for a moment, then said, "With the girl's parents. I want to know the particulars of her death. That might shed some light on why she was buried above a secret network of tunnels."

When Ravenwood turned his back on the inspector to collect his coat, an image flashed across his mind's eye. Something struck him in the back of the head a moment later, and Ravenwood turned. The inspector was throwing peanuts at his head.

"You just can't leave my life or my work alone, can you?" Stagg asked, utterly exasperated.

Ravenwood shrugged. "It's my favorite hobby."

"I can arrest you."

"I can make bail."

"I could shoot you."

"So could I. Know why I don't?"

"My life is incomplete not knowing that," he said, thick on the sarcasm.

"Because my life is more entertaining if I get to mess with yours." He reached for his coat, and found that it wasn't on the police block like he'd left it. Instead, it was in the hands of a young, fresh-faced officer in blue.

He offered it quickly. "It fell, so I held onto it so it wouldn't fall again."

"Nice of you," Ravenwood said, and took it. Ravenwood's hand made contact with the officer's for only a half second, but it sent an electric shock up his arm. It was painful, and Ravenwood recoiled. He hadn't been prepared for that.

"You're burning daylight," Stagg said immediately, seeming not to notice. "Come on."

He hoisted his Luger and squeezed the trigger.

"Huh?" Ravenwood was still shocked by the contact. He didn't know what to make of it—the energy that had come off the young officer was a dark kind of energy, and it stuck to the skin and the soul like impermeable ink.

Stagg shoved him away from the grave, "Stop playing, and move your ass."

Ravenwood tried to look at the young officer before Stagg pushed him along, but the young man had turned his back on the Inspector and Ravenwood.

"Who was that cop holding my coat?"

"New guy. How should I know every uniform that walks the streets of my city?"

Ravenwood let it go with the inspector, but that was it. The young man raised questions, and those questions needed answers.

"Where do the victim's parents live?" Ravenwood asked as he climbed into his car and the Inspector walked over to the black and white cruiser.

"About two blocks from the Sussex Towers."

"Then I'll race you there."

He dropped behind the wheel, fired up the racing-tuned engine and tore away from the curb. Ravenwood was to the end of the block and turning east before Stagg had gotten the cruiser fired up and in gear. Ravenwood laughed when he heard the siren wail, and grabbed another gear for the race across town.

✳ ✳ ✳

Ravenwood had stopped off at his own place long enough to grab a clean suit, wash his face and run a comb through his hair. That done, he met Stagg over at the address for Mr. and Mrs. Jacob Abrams.

In the elevator, riding to the twelfth floor, Stagg had made one thing very clear—he was not to be interrupted in his line of questioning. They'd run through the basic story as necessary for Ravenwood, but that was it. He was all about causing the family as little harm as they possibly could.

"That's awfully noble of you, Horatio," Ravenwood said with an honest smile.

"I will shoot you," Stagg snapped, "And no one will blame me for it."

"You don't mean that." The elevator dinged, and Ravenwood gestured to the crimson carpeted hallway. "Shall we?"

The hall was adorned with dark wood paneling, a lightly painted ceiling, and brass fixtures for all the major things that people touched like knobs and railings. The doors were made out of gold-accented, dark mahogany.

Stagg knocked twice, gently, and waited. Ravenwood heard the footsteps approach, and then the door was pulled open gently.

"Inspector?" Mrs. Abrams asked, uncertain of herself. "What are you doing here?"

"Can I come in, Maria? I need to talk to you and your husband."

"Yes, of course," she stood aside, and Stagg stepped inside slowly. He pulled his fedora off, and Ravenwood did the same. The younger man took the inspector's hat and hung it on the mirror-laden bureau in the front hallway.

"Jacob," Maria Abrams said, "It's Inspector Stagg."

"What does he want?" the husband snapped. "He didn't help us before. What can he do now?"

"That's not fair, Jacob!" Maria said in her unusually high-pitched, girlish voice. "He's done everything he can for us."

"You catch my daughter's killer yet?" Jacob asked harshly. He was the exact contrast to the fair skinned and petite Mrs. Abrams. Jacob Abrams was tall, broad shoulder and hard-jawed. At one point in his life he possessed immense strength, but all that strength now went into containing the rage he felt at the injustice done to his family. That was evidenced by the drinker's shake to his hands, the gnarled knuckles, and the beer belly.

"When he puts a bullet in my daughter's killer, that'll be everything he can do."

"It's not out of the realm of possibilities," Stagg decided, then took a seat in a small armchair. Ravenwood stood, and decided to walk around a little bit. He'd hear everything clearly enough, even if he was on the opposite end of the apartment. It was about a thousand square feet—quite a set up considering how expensive this place was.

Ravenwood made a mental note, where's the money come from?

"What happened?" Maria asked.

"It seems that someone vandalized your daughter's grave."

Ravenwood heard a sharp sob catch in the mother's throat, and she sighed, "Why? Why can't my little girl just rest in peace?"

"We don't know," Stagg said quietly. "But this case is my top priority."

"Now it is," Jacob growled. "What about when she was killed? You couldn't be bothered then."

"There were bodies all over the place," Stagg said angrily. "And I had to put a killer to them all—do you have any idea how hard that is?"

"I don't give a damn!" Jacob roared. "You never found my daughter's killer, and now you expect me to be gracious to you? You owe us everything, and you don't even have the decency to admit you screwed up!"

"Gentleman," Ravenwood tapped the end of the walking stick hard on the floor, enough to make the boards rattle. "Let us focus on the task at hand. You can kill each other after the job of catching your daughter's assassin is done."

"Yes," Stagg agreed. "I'll personally put the pistol in your hand if you really wanna cross that bridge."

"Count on it." Jacob Abrams leaned back in his chair, temporarily appeased. "What do you want?"

Stagg opened his mouth to ask something but Ravenwood stepped in, holding a picture of the girl in question, Monica, standing next to a boy in a suit. "Who is this young man?"

"Andrew," Maria said dreamily. "My baby girl loved him."

"He was no good for her," Jacob snarled. "He was always calling her at the strangest hours, never gave me a straight answer about anything he did."

"What kind of things did he say?"

"That he was a scientist, or some such. He said he was working with on a cure for something, I don't remember what."

"And his name was Andrew?"

"Yes, Andrew Sinclair."

Ravenwood wrote it down, and walked into the bedroom areas. At the end of the thick carpeted hallway were three doors. The one on the left was open, and showed a king-sized bed, presumably the Abrams' bed. The door on the right was closed, and the door in front was open part way.

He walked into what once was Monica's bedroom. He looked around slowly, noting the way that they'd kept everything undisturbed since her death. It was a shame, actually, because it was unhealthy. The dead are gone, he reflected, and can't be called back with any great success. Even talking to them is frowned upon, as he was taught by the monks of Tibet.

He tapped his stick against the floor. His skin tingled like there was an electrical charge in the air—similar to what he felt from the suited policeman earlier today. Ravenwood walked slowly around the room, wondering if the energy had a specific source. He found it a moment later, in the dresser. He knelt to pull open the bottom drawer, where something hidden would most likely reside, and the glass of the window to the left exploded inward.

He threw himself flat to the floor as the shot echoed across the street.

"Stagg!" he yelled. "We've got a problem!"

There was a woman's scream down the hallway, followed by the grunt of a man in pain.

"Stay down!" Stagg ordered. Ravenwood rolled onto his stomach and crawled over to the wall. He stood up slowly, just out of sight from the window, and stepped carefully over to it. There was a man on the adjoining rooftop, a rifle in his hands. He was firing at the apartment. Ravenwood shoved the Luger out in front of him, angled the barrel up to compensate for bullet drop, and squeezed the trigger twice.

The thunder that erupted from the barrel filled the room and echoed between the buildings. The first slug smashed into the concrete ten feet low, and the second sent up sparks into the face of the shooter. He dropped out of sight and Ravenwood shouted, "Call your hounds, Stagg!"

He sprinted through the door of the bedroom, through the front door, and found the stairwell that would lead downstairs. He sped down the stairs three at a time.

He slammed through the lower door to the lobby and raced out into the street. The shooter, wearing a fedora low over his eyes, ran towards a waiting convertible Chevrolet. He threw himself into it as Ravenwood staggered to a stop. He aimed the Luger, and fired two shots. The first hit the metal, sending up sparks, and the second smashed into the shoulder of the driver. He screamed and fell forward against the steering wheel, holding his arm.

Ravenwood sprinted across the street, but his mind's eye was blinded by a vision of him recoiling backwards, blackness consuming his consciousness—aware of nothing as death took him.

He faltered, and went to his hands and knees as a shot roared from the direction of the car. The engine roared, and the car raced away from the building. Ravenwood stood up slowly, his hands trembling.

Stagg was heaving and out of breath when he got to the street. He had his police-issue .38 caliber gun in one hand.

"What happened?"

"He got away. But I hit the driver."

"Car?"

Ravenwood tapped his temple "I got it."

"Telephone inside," he continued. "Get it on the wires as fast as you can, Stagg! We might still be able to catch these guys."

Ravenwood limped back inside, his knee skinned where he'd fallen. He passed his Ford, and looked down at it. The shot that would've killed him missed his body—but it didn't miss the Ford. There was a small leak of oil from the back side of the exposed engine compartment. He sighed.

"Perfect," he muttered, and stabbed the engine with his walking stick. "Just bloody perfect."

✳ ✳ ✳

Ravenwood felt exhausted when he'd finally been able to drag himself back to his penthouse at the Sussex Towers. He'd walked back, because the NYPD had towed his car.

So when he finally climbed the seven marble steps to the front door and walked past the upper door-man named Stephen, he wasn't exactly expecting Lilly Collins to be standing there in pumps, a pinstripe pantsuit with a dark blue fedora on. She's a freelance journalist, a damn good one too.

"Someone divine must really hate me today." He approached her quickly and said, "The NYPD will answer any questions you may have."

"No they won't," she countered. "And I want answers, not 'no comments.'"

"Sounds like a personal problem. I'm not qualified to provide insight to NYPD operations."

"That's fine because I don't want NYPD insight. I want your insight."

He rolled his eyes. "Go away, Lilly."

"That's a rude way to treat a lady," she pouted. "And I was gonna help you on your case, too."

He stopped, knowing she was baiting her. He had no other ideas about how to proceed, anyway. The shooter was gone, and the police were fumbling the search for the car. Jacob Abrams was dead, silenced by the gunman. Ravenwood had no idea where Maria Abrams had gone. He didn't even really know where to start with regards to the books on the shelves in the sacrificial chamber.

"I need some lunch," he said. "I'll buy, you'll talk."

"My kind of date. I heard your car got shot up."

He glared at her. "Do not mock my Ford."

"Right. I'll drive. Where are we eating?"

"Marlowe's." It was one of the best restaurants in Manhattan, and one of the most exclusive. He never had any trouble getting a table, though.

She led him outside, hips gyrating while she walked. She was acutely aware of the shape of her body, and used it as a weapon just as efficiently as a soldier uses a rifle. Ravenwood suspected that she liked that feeling of power.

The car was almost as special as the driver. It was a Cord 810 soft-top with a straight-eight motor, two-hundred-fifty horsepower, and a small armory in the back seat. The bench folded down to reveal a variety of guns for any situation. He looked at her strangely, and gestured to the hidden armory.

"A girl's gotta protect herself."

"Uh-huh."

She smiled disarmingly, but it didn't work on Ravenwood. "Just drive." He leaned back. He didn't sleep, just rested his eyes.

Marlowe's was half a mile from the Sussex Towers. It was a first-floor restaurant with broad glass windows on the outside wall, a pair of double doors with a well-dressed door-man to open them for you, and a maitre-d standing just inside, eager to please. Ravenwood led Lilly inside, and said, "Good afternoon, Desmond."

"Mr. Ravenwood, what table would you like?"

"A quiet one in a corner. If you don't mind."

"Not at all, sir, this way please."

He led them into the back end of the restaurant, near the kitchen. "Will this do?"

Ravenwood nodded, and put a twenty dollar bill in the man's hand, "Yes, thank you."

Desmond bowed, and walked off. Lilly shrugged out of her coat and hung it on the peg next to the wooden wall of the booth, and slid inside. She put her notebook on the table. Ravenwood sat across from her. "Well?" he asked. "What's on your mind?"

"No coffee first? Just straight to business?"

"Yup. Straight to it."

"So where shall I start?"

"At the beginning, I should think."

She smiled. "I was a reporter at the New York *Sun Times* when Monica Abrams was murdered. I did a few small stories on it, since all the bigger papers had the real scoops. The cops wouldn't give me the time of day." She shrugged innocently. "I had to use other means to gain access to the scenes to see for myself what had happened."

"And?"

"I discovered something. I kept it to myself because I'm not naïve enough to think anyone would believe me, at least, not until I saw you."

He rolled his eyes. "Get to the point, please."

"The girl was killed in the center of a symbol, made from poured lead."

That grabbed his attention. "From what?"

"Molten lead. It was a concrete floor, and there was a seven-sided symbol around her, poured in lead, like someone had a huge vat of it and just poured it out in this shape." Lilly drew quickly on her small notebook, then twisted it around for Ravenwood to see. He knew the symbol even before she was done drawing it.

"An alchemist's circle," he said absently. "Why was she killed in an alchemist's circle?"

It was a seven-pointed star, but the points of the star were uneven. However, when drawn properly, it created a perfectly even seven-sided heptagon in the center. She was killed in the center.

"Okay," he said softly. "This is starting to make sense." It was only a vague sensation of starting to see the bigger picture, but it felt good to have a firm grasp on something.

"Can you explain this to me, Ravenwood? Because, frankly, I don't get it."

"Alchemy was the first science. When it began, it was viewed as magical and thus heresy by the church, and anyone found practicing alchemy would be put to death. But many kept at it, kept learning and divining its secrets. There are two parts to it. The first is the magical side, which believes that any energy in the universe can be transformed into a different kind of energy through rituals. At one point, water to steam through heat, was thought to be magic."

"But that's science."

"Exactly, like so many things, what once appeared to be magic is merely a reaction of some sort. And the other end of things was a proper, hard science, like chemistry, biology, and such."

"Now what?"

"I don't really know. Alchemy is such an unpopular focus as far as science today is concerned because most of the early experiments were so crude." Ravenwood leaned back and scratched his chin.

"But you think something different, don't you?"

"I think that there's a line between science and religion, and I think that whoever's doing these things has found a way to merge the two for a specifically intended result."

"Spooky."

"You have no idea."

"So what do you do now? You have to stop them, you know."

"Stop whom?" Ravenwood asked skeptically. "There is no name to those who've used disused tunnels under a graveyard for sacrifices, or those who murder innocent bystanders to keep them silent. It's almost like a mafia, some sick and twisted crime family."

"You know they're alchemists, right?" she said. "So how do you find them?"

Ravenwood pulled out the journals he had been given from the old woman who'd woken him this morning and from the sacrificial chamber beneath the cemetery. The same seven-sided symbol was on the cover, and he shook his head.

"There isn't a directory for secret scientists doing strange rites on the living," he said, then he tapped the journals. "But there may be someone who could serve that purpose."

"Who's that?"

"He lives in the warehouse district. That's also where he works."

"Where who works?" she asked as the coffee was delivered. He hesitated while she poured some milk and a spoonful of sugar into the steaming saucer, and let her take a sip.

"Professor Wallace Edenton, better known as Professor Johnny."

She gagged on it and set the cup down with a cough, moaning and coughing. Ravenwood laughed quietly.

"When you're done, we'll leave."

"I'm good." She pushed her coffee back. "But you get to walk there."

"Okay. I'll tell Professor Johnny that you said hello."

"No talking while I drink, okay?" She glared at him.

Ravenwood nodded, and drank his own coffee.

✳ ✳ ✳

Professor Johnny's laboratory was in a dingy looking warehouse building in the lower west side of Manhattan. It looked like every other building on the street, and no one would suspect that it housed one of the greatest scientific intellects since Isaac Newton.

Lilly brought the Cord to a stop across the street.

"Why not park in front? There's room…"

She was interrupted by the sound of something electric spooling up. There was a flash of furious blue light and then all the windows of the building exploded outward, lighting shooting into the street, absorbing into metal objects, blowing out the street lights. People screamed and rushed away from the building, staring at it in terror. Ravenwood laughed quietly.

"Any more questions?"

She shook her head slowly, "Holy crap."

"That is Professor Johnny," he said, gestured through the broken windows on the ground floor of the warehouse. A tall man was running madly back and forth between several large machines. His blonde hair was standing on end, he had black soot stains on his face, and his goggles looked cracked. Ravenwood crossed the street and leaned against one of the broken windows.

"It didn't work so well, Professor!" Ravenwood said.

"It worked brilliantly!" the scientist argued. "I just have to make a note never to turn it up to level five."

"Turn what up?"

"Come in and I'll show you!"

The front door of the metal walled warehouse was made of thick iron with steel bars reinforcing it.

Ravenwood laughed as he shoved through the door. The basement looked like a World War I trench. Nicola Tesla owed many of his most brilliant electrical processes to the scientist standing before Ravenwood and Lilly. The professor had an assistant, leaned up against one wall. The young man looked wounded.

"Professor!" Ravenwood shouted, "Tend to your—"

"You're alright, aren't you, Nathan?" Professor Johnny asked, not looking at Nate. "Just a flesh wound, ya?"

"Part of the ricochet hit me," the assistant muttered.

"How do you feel?" Now Johnny turned, and looked at him intently. The younger man shrugged.

"My insides feel liquefied."

The professor started kicking debris around, looking for something specific, and suddenly found it. He hoisted a peculiar device, and carried it over to the young man. He held it up and clicked it on. "It looks like you took quite a shock. Did you wear the insulating vest?"

Nathan Boroughs nodded slowly, and tore open his coat. Underneath was a copper wired vest that had wires running off it into a stack of black cases.

Professor Johnny slid over to the black cases, "We've got a huge amount of power now, kids!" he had an English accent, though his assistant was American. He laughed, and slapped the pack of batteries, "Now, what'd you need my friend?"

"I needed to talk to you about some alchemists."

"Talk kindly," Professor Johnny laughed. "I am one."

"It looks like you took quite a shock."

"You're a maniac," Nathan said.

"You're just cross because you caught the ricochet."

"You forgot to mention how much it would hurt."

"Yes, well, now we know." He smiled.

"What was the plan?" Ravenwood asked.

"I'm developing a pistol that can stun a person into harmlessness. But it doesn't just have one setting, because different situations call for different levels of force!" He laughed, and kicked debris around further looking for the device. He shrieked, "Ah ha!" He snatched it up and held it in the air proudly. "This is it!"

"How's it work?" Ravenwood poked at some of the debris with his walking stick.

"Quite carefully," he said, "Look here—"

"We don't have time for this," Lilly said.

"Says you," Professor Johnny said pointedly. "There's always time for a gizmo."

Ravenwood took the gun in his hand. It had a significant amount of heft. There was a wooden grip, a large metal trigger, with a large cylinder on top. The middle chamber was made of glass, and seemed to house a liquid. The front chamber tapered to a point, and was made of copper. The back chamber was made of a denser metal, with a dial on the side with numbers going from 0-5 with hash marks in between the numbers.

"This is a small battery that can hold a great deal of power and funnel it into the central chamber, which is full of salt water. The last chamber is the firing mechanism, and it shoots the electricity at the target."

"What's the range?" Ravenwood asked.

"No more than two dozen paces at level two. Any more, and you risk killing the person you're shooting."

"Can I borrow it?"

"That's why it's in your hand, boyo." He slapped Ravenwood on the shoulder. "Now, what can I do for you?"

"Alchemists. The dark kind."

"The ones who mix ritual sacrifice with their sciences?" Professor Johnny shuddered. "I hate those buggers. Damn evil blokes, if you ask me."

"We need to find ones who've been doing this kind of work." Ravenwood passed the professor the journals. "And if you can, tell us what the end goal is."

"Oh dearie me," he said sadly. "This isn't good at all, lad." With a great sweep of his arms, he cleared off his desk and spread out the journals. He began flipping through them quickly glancing over things faster than most folks could've fathomed. He was making notes with a piece of chalk on the board behind the desk.

"First, you tell me everything that's transpired since you laid your mitts on these books, eh? I can't get a full picture of what's what until you tell me that much."

Ravenwood leaned against a concrete support pillar and started the story. He began with being roused from his sleep to talk to the old widower who threw the knife at him, the same woman whom he couldn't predict anything about. Johnny made a note about that on the chalkboard, but even Ravenwood couldn't make out what the mark meant.

He explained the incidents at the graveyard, including the trap-door coffin that led to underground tunnels with the sacrificial chamber and the second alchemist's notebook. He concluded with being in the apartment of the Abramses, and Jacob being killed.

For a long moment, silence fell over the broad warehouse. No one moved, and the only sound that could be heard was the odd moan of pain from Nathan.

"What was being done in those tunnels?"

"Specifically? Women were being murdered on that table."

"In what way, I mean. Did you get specific details, or was it just someone carving them up?"

"My impression was that someone was doing a very specific procedure. There was a great deal of blood on that table."

The professor nodded slowly. He scratched at his chin ponderously. At length, he said, "I don't know what to make of the overall situation at present except to say two things. First, I'd look at those tunnels a little closer. They run all over New York City, and they're a lot easier to access than you'd think."

"Through the sewers and such?"

"Precisely." Professor Johnny tapped the side of his nose.

"What am I looking for?"

"More of what you've been finding. Someone is using those tunnels for a business. Look for the employees."

"That's brilliant," Lilly complimented.

"You sound surprised," the Professor said, looking like he was actually wounded by the words. Ravenwood smirked.

"What was the second thing?"

"The only sect of alchemists I know that uses this combines the worst effects of both science and black magic is the Hellfire Club. This stuff is soul-eating work, boyo. Whatever guardian angels you've got looking out for you will need to pull extra shifts."

"Anything else?"

"Keep me updated."

"Would you like to come along?" the Stepson of Mystery suggested.

"I thought you'd never ask." The young professor's eyes got misty.

"Oh goody," Nathan groaned, then shrugged off the vest slowly. He looked much better when it was off his body. He cracked his neck and said, "What'll we need?"

"Our coats and our guns. That'll be it, I should think."

"And the journals," Ravenwood added.

"Where do we begin?" Lilly inquired.

"An abandoned church up on 19th and Alameda," Professor Johnny replied. "A scientist I had correspondences with once, many years ago, had moved in there for his work. The building was supposedly condemned, but no one wanted to build on that ground, so he kept it."

"What are we expecting there?"

"The walking dead, demons of an unmentionable evil, and scientists who are quite mad."

"Just another day at the office," Ravenwood deadpanned.

"Pretty much, yes, boyo. We'll take the truck." The truck was a converted police-issue arrest wagon. It had the rails in the back to attach handcuffs and chains to, but it also had several boxes housing various pieces of equipment, most of which were built by the professor.

"Nathan, do you mind if I drive?"

"I think the whole city would like you to never drive again, Professor."

"Then make it so." Professor Johnny marched regally over the passenger door. Ravenwood climbed into the back, and offered a hand to Lilly—who promptly ignored it and climbed into the wagon.

"You make it hard for a man to be a gentleman."

"That's my intent." She had a seductive squint in her eyes. Ravenwood sat down across from her.

"Can I ask you something?" she started.

"You just did."

She continued like he hadn't spoken. The truck rattled out onto the street, and began the journey up to the top of the city where the abandoned church was located.

"The cops who've worked with you in the past say you've got strange powers. Occult powers."

"Is there a question in there?"

"Do you have mystical powers or not?"

"I have an innate sense of observation, but I don't think that's mystical. I do, however, have an ability to predict things if I focus on them intently. With that focus, I can predict their actions, their speech too sometimes. As for them being 'occult powers,' well, that's a different story entirely."

He leaned back and crossed his legs. He adjusted the expensive cotton trousers so he was sitting comfortably, and rested the walking stick across his lap.

"Occult is simply Latin for 'hidden,' and thus anything that is hidden from the naked eye can be referred to as 'occult.' What it is, and what people reference it to be, are very different things entirely. Professor Johnny mentioned one when he talked of the Hellfire Club. It's an old hermetic society, which also means secret."

"What do they do?"

"They seek control in any way they deem necessary. Fear is a powerful manipulation tool, and these kinds of people have never hesitated to apply that power to achieve their own ends."

"Such as?"

"Say an arch-duke gets shot by an obscure person. But these two pawns belong to larger authorities, like Germany and Russia. So they declare war on each other. Other countries that allied with the initial two get drawn into the fracas, and before you know it, we've got the Great War."

"How do you know this?" Lilly pressed. He deflected.

"Also, suppose that the person who shot the arch-duke wasn't Russian at all, but was actually an Anglo-Saxon man whose task was to start a war. The fuse is set. It just needs to be lighted."

"Is that what's at work here?"

"It's entirely possible," Ravenwood decided. "But I don't know who the players are. I'm absolutely certain of the Hellfire Club. The symbol on the cover of those journals is a combination of the alchemist's triangle and the Hellfire Club's official seal, which is the upside-down cross inside a pentagram."

"So now what?"

"We go to the church and take a look around. I hope it answers some questions because I've got too many of them bouncing around in my head right now."

"Like what?"

"What work was being done in that crypt beneath the cemetery? What purpose is served in killing Jacob Abrams? Who killed him? Why was his daughter's grave disturbed? Who is behind this? Most importantly, what's their end game?"

"Those are heavy questions."

"Good thing I've got broad shoulders."

"So if your powers aren't evil, like the stuff that the Hellfire Club deals in, then what is it?"

"I spent a great deal of time in the mountains near Tibet studying with monks." He held the stick up. "And they taught me a great many things. Energy is everywhere, and harnessing that energy through meditation grants power that appears to be preternatural."

"That's a load of crap," she said. "There's no such thing as psychics and stuff."

"Men who can look into a mind like it were an open book and see anything? No, I don't believe that." He leaned back then planted both feet on the floor. He put the stick across the tops of his knees and gripped it tightly. "But I can show you."

"How?"

"Think of something that only you know that no one else on earth could possibly know. When you think of it, nod at me, then decide to say it, but do not speak."

"Anyone can finish my sentence if they're clever about it."

"I'll finish the sentence before you even speak it." He smiled.

She leaned back and crossed her legs, then her arms giving him a skeptical expression.

"Do it," he urged, "and tell me if I'm wrong."

"Okay fine," she said, then focused for a moment. He could see it in her eyes when she thought of something. It was heavy, whatever it was, and he could see that simply by looking at her. He felt the aura around her get heavy, like a weight had been laid across her shoulders. That's the way this stuff worked. Whatever was on the forefront of one's mind was transmitted through the energy inside every human being. If one paid attention, one could pick up on those auras, and read them, understand them.

"Your mother was killed by your father," he revealed quietly.

"I wasn't ready." Her eyes jerked straight up to him and she glared at him with brutal hatred.

"It's what you were thinking," he shrugged, "and no one but you knew that he did it. The police thought it was an accident, wrote it off. But you knew the truth. You were fifteen at the time."

"Stop," she whispered.

"You spent two more years in that house, earning his trust slowly, making him believe that you were on his side, convincing him that you two were peas in a pod. So when the day finally came, you killed him too."

"Stop it now, or I'll—"

"Except when that day came, you were talking about the night your mother had died, about her 'accident' and for a moment you hesitated. You almost believed the lie you'd held up for the past two years."

He tapered off, and then looked her in the eye. A tear ran down her face and her fists were shaking with rage.

"How?" she hissed. "How could you know all that?"

He smiled weakly, and ran a hand over his slicked back hair, and explained the process of a person's aura, and the link between what they're thinking about and what can be read from the things projected into that aura.

Her fists were still knotted up with uncontrollable anger as she struggled to put a noose on it.

"Don't hold it back," he advised. "You've held it back too long as it is."

She shoved off the bench and lunged at him. He didn't move to stop her as the first punch landed across his jaw. He felt the sting, knew immediately that she'd drawn blood. She hooked her other hand across the other side of his mouth and he tasted blood. The third hit was aimed for his nose, and he grabbed her fist in mid-flight. He said very quietly, "Take that rage, and aim it at the people we're trying to stop."

"The people you're trying to stop didn't just read my mind and tell me the story of my mother's murder."

"Didn't they? Didn't they do this to someone else? They buried a girl alive for their experiments, for the purpose of finding a pawn to sacrifice to start another war. They've killed a man who's only goal for two and half years was seeing justice done on his daughter's killer. They've robbed a mother of her husband and her daughter. You've been fighting these men your entire life."

He pushed her back gently and set her back on the bench. He let go of her hands slowly.

"I'm not the enemy." He looked out the back of the truck, and noted that the scenery had changed to look very similar to the neighborhood where he'd seen the crazy old woman, Mrs. Langston, yesterday morning.

"You and I are going to settle this when we're done," she promised.

"Whatever settling that needs doing is between you and your

conscience," he explained. "Your subconscious threw up those events, not your conscious mind. The former is almost always more powerful than the latter when it comes to facts of the heart and soul."

"I hate you so much," she growled.

"Be that as it may, you still threw the story out there."

"You could've sounded less like some emotionless pig when you said it."

"I had no control over the tone that I delivered the story. I was telling the story exactly the way you tell it to yourself when you need to comfort your own conscience over your actions."

"He was laughing when he died," she whispered. "He was happy. He was genuinely happy." Her body was here in the truck with Ravenwood, but it didn't take any of his skill to see that her mind wasn't. "I could still taste the blood in my mouth from where I'd bitten my cheek when he'd hit me. Maybe if I'd—"

"Stop there," he said harshly and leaned forward. "There was nothing that you could have done to change him. There was nothing on earth; nothing short of a miracle intervention from God could've saved that man's soul."

"He was my father."

"The bloodiest demons we ever fight are usually closest to home. And that's just the way it is."

"Oh yeah?" she scoffed. "What personal demons of your own have you got?"

The truck lurched over a heavy bump, and the brakes squealed as it started to come to a stop. He shrugged, "Every day I have to fight to control my abilities. I'm seeing more at once, with less focus."

"And how is that bad?'

"I don't want to be in people's heads," he confessed. "Some days I wish I could just live normally, like the newspapers would have you believe. What happens when I can't differentiate between what's in a person's heart and what the eye can see? What I can do is nothing to desire, Lilly, believe me."

The truck jolted to a stop, and Nathan banged on the dividing metal bulkhead between the cab and the cargo area.

"We're here."

✳ ✳ ✳

Ravenwood undid the strap that kept the Luger from falling out of the holster. He undid his coat, and then tapped the end of the walking stick against the ground. He shuddered at the energy that flowed up the stick to his hand and up his arm.

Evil inhabited this place, from the top of the granite spire to the subbasements that would house the ancient dead. It scared him. There was a sense of finality to this place, to the events that had been set in motion a scant eighteen hours ago. It felt like it had been longer.

Professor Johnny walked around the front of the truck and said, "I've been going over these notebooks, and I've got a better idea what's going on."

"Tell me after you see everything inside."

"What do you see?" Johnny asked seriously.

"I don't know what, or whom, but I know that one way or another, this is where it ends."

"Once more into the breach, dear friends?" Professor Johnny said.

Ravenwood nodded, and Nathan hauled back the bolt on the Thompson submachine-gun. He said, "Not if I've got anything to say about it."

"I knew there was a reason I brought you along," the Professor said happily.

"It ain't for my good looks and charming personality."

"No, but those qualities are always so very welcome," Johnny said honestly, and began stomping up towards the granite steps of the small cathedral. Ravenwood grabbed his arm to stop him. The professor didn't protest.

The night was cold and humidity hung thick in the air. The trees in the cemetery yards off to the left were rustling ominously, and cast unpredictable shadows across the grounds. The only light were a few dim streetlights half a block away from the church. They had battery powered flashlights and lanterns, but those weren't very reassuring.

Ravenwood didn't carry a lantern and walked out in front of the group. As they got closer to the church building, they could see that it was leaning in on itself. It was like the weight of the evil that had absorbed the whole plot of land was pulling the church down on itself.

This was once a hallowed place. Ravenwood could still feel the remnants of that holy energy in the ground. He absorbed it easily and willingly, drew it to him like small streams of water flowing downhill into a river. Knowing that there was still some good in this place gave him confidence, helped push back some of the fear.

The darkness hadn't consumed everything here.

He approached the front steps slowly. He could perceive the inside of the church, the pews and the dirty, cracked stain glass windows. He could sense the red candles and the symbols drawn around the central altar with melted red candles. An evil entity lurked at the back of the church.

He climbed the steps, and at the top there was a creak in the granite he stood on, and the block shifted. The sound of crows shrieking ripped across the night and jarred Ravenwood. He saw the black shapes slicing across the sky, but in that instant he moaned in agony.

His knees went weak and he collapsed down to one knee. He felt like a brick wall had just been slammed down across his head, and someone was hammering spikes into his brain. He felt a stab of agony and a terrible, ancient voice rang in his ears, "I will kill you." And then the presence disappeared.

He groaned, and the pain began to lessen. In its place was a void that could not be filled, an unfathomable darkness that could not be penetrated. He felt blind, deaf, to what was inside now.

"Mate?" Professor Johnny asked quietly. "What happened?"

"I can't see inside," he said, "I can't see anything."

"We'll be alright," Johnny said. "I've got faith."

Ravenwood looked, and in the hand that held the lantern was a set of crimson colored beads and a small crucifix. Ravenwood nodded to the professor.

He stood up slowly, and started for the front doors. He pushed the first aside slowly with his shoulder. As the door swung open, he lifted the Luger and swept through the darkness. His eyes came to rest on the altar. Based on what he'd sensed, he expected to see a giant, shimmering serpent.

What he saw instead was a well-lit church. The candles were concentrated heavily near the front, but they illuminated nearly every corner except the back door that guarded the entrance to the crypts.

Ravenwood lifted the pistol slowly, and looked around the back of the church again, this time looking for more specific details. The candles only illuminated so much, and he knew nothing could hide entirely from his field of vision.

The furious buzzing of electricity hummed from the back of the church, and then a streak of blue lighting shot out from the top of the bronze crown of thorns on the statue of the crucifixion. It shrieked across the church as Ravenwood threw himself down into cover between two rotted pews. The electricity buried into a receptor at the entrance, and the doors shut with a brutal slam.

"Why must you keep pushing?" a man's voice cried from the lighted altar. "We weren't ready, but you've forced our hand!" it sounded like the voice he'd just heard in his ears, threatening his life.

"What are you doing, precisely? Maybe I can help," Ravenwood said,

"Mate? What happened?"

and started crawling beneath the pews. The voice laughed angrily.

"You'll see for yourself when I'm done here."

"I hate how that sounds," Lilly whispered.

"That's a clever device," Professor Johnny said. "Very nifty indeed."

"Ogle on it later, Professor," Nathan said. Ravenwood watched him push the Professor to safety off to one side of the pews, the Thompson in his hands.

Ravenwood rolled between two rows, and sat up slowly. He stole a glance over the edge of the bench. The man who activated the electricity wore a white robe with the seven-sided symbol in crimson. It didn't take any great stretch of the imagination to know it was blood. He had a rifle in his hands, and when he spotted Ravenwood, he fired at him.

Ravenwood ducked as something smashed into the backrest of the pew. He looked at it, and then hauled it out of the wood. It was a bullet-shaped dart, the modern equivalent of the poison tipped arrow.

Ravenwood scrambled under the pews. The dart rifle barked again, and Ravenwood threw himself upright. He aimed at the man with the white cloak and fired rapidly from the Luger.

The man twisted and ducked behind the altar. Ravenwood shoved to the left to get around the pew, and raced up towards the altar. The man in the cloak stood up again, "Don't do it!" Ravenwood shouted. He aimed at the man in the cloak. The man fired, and the dart hit Ravenwood in the chest. He fired twice and both 9mm slugs caught the cloaked man in the upper chest. He staggered and went down.

Ravenwood wrenched the dart out of his chest, and staggered over to the fallen man. He hauled the hood back and exposed his face to the light.

It was Jacob Abrams!

"Why are you doing this?"

The man coughed, blood spattered across his lips. He shook his head slowly, "You can't understand..."

"Was your daughter really murdered?" Ravenwood shook the man hard. "Was she really dead?"

"She was buried alive by a crooked cop. The same man hired the sniper who tried to kill me at home. Stagg didn't know any better, thought I was dead. I let him think that. Maria helped sell it to him."

"Your wife is involved?"

"This was her idea," he coughed, and a rivulet of blood slid down the side of his face from his mouth. "It was her idea to start this work. She told me about the church, about the crazy scientist living here. He had a wonderful idea."

"What was the idea?" Ravenwood said. His head was getting foggy, his eyes were losing their ability to focus.

"To start a war. To purge the corruption in this city. It would start here and cleanse outward."

"How would you do it?"

Abrams was getting weaker. Ravenwood was a good shot, and he hit the man center-mass. His lungs were filling with blood, and he was close to death now.

"Fear," he said. "We'd use fear to start the war."

"How?" Ravenwood roared. The darkness was settling in around his eyes, and he was struggling to keep a straight thought.

"We'd put something in the water, something that would free the spirits within everyone, make them see the world more clearly like we do," he sighed. "It is going to be beautiful."

And then he died. Ravenwood shuddered. His hands started to shake, and rage boiled up in his stomach. He started growling, he couldn't stop himself. The rage overwhelmed his eyes, and he roared in agony. He dropped to his knees as Professor Johnny asked, "What's wrong with you."

Ravenwood's eyes snapped over to the blonde professor and a vague voice in his head rumbled, "Find control."

He leaned forward and leapt into a sprint. He'd claw out the professor's eyes, rip his throat out, disembowel him, he'd cause him so much pain.

The blow that took him sideways was absolutely unforeseen. He stumbled to the right and went down hard, sliding into the pew.

"He's out of his mind!" Professor Johnny yelled. "Bring him out of it!"

"How?" Nathan asked.

"Pain, overwhelming pain would burn this out of his system with adrenaline!"

Ravenwood couldn't hear them anymore; he could only see the professor, only knew that he had to kill him. He was the only one who could stop what was coming. He shoved to his feet and rushed at him again, this time trying to tackle him. Again, he was thrown sideways, this time he slid all the way to the altar. He landed hard on his back, and knocked over several candle stands.

One fell on his neck and the burning flame and the boiling wax burned him. He roared in agony and for an instant the fog around his eyes lifted, but only for a moment. Then he was sprinting at the professor, all control lost.

He saw a shape step in front of the professor. The shape lunged, tackled Ravenwood. He was only vaguely aware that he couldn't move his arms, or get to his feet. Ravenwood screamed, tried to throw the shape off. There was shouting around him, and a moment later the enormous pain of fire was brought down on the backs of his arms. He screamed in agony as the darkness around his eyes receded. He went limp with exhaustion, and the flames were removed. He could smell something burning, knew only in the back of his mind that it was actually his own flesh.

"Nathan, Lilly, to the basement with you," the professor ordered.

"I have to go too," Ravenwood mumbled. He tried to move, found himself unable to.

"You're in no shape..." Professor Johnny argued.

"Bugger off, Professor." He took a slow breath and began to move his arms. Nathan was still holding him down.

"I'm alright, Boroughs," Ravenwood said.

"Let him up, lad," Professor Johnny instructed. Nathan got up slowly and Ravenwood followed. He was unsteady, but he knew now exactly what to do.

"Lilly, go for help. Get Stagg, tell him everything and bring him down here."

"What are you going to do?"

"The professor, Nathan and I are going below. The only way out is through that door, so no one will get past us. We'll stop the scientist and Mrs. Abrams, and the professor will put an end to this work."

"Yes," agreed the professor. "What he said."

"Are you certain?"

"No," Ravenwood picked up his walking stick. The good energy that he'd felt earlier flowed into him and purged what remained of the shadows. "But it's a plan."

Lilly stepped up to him, put a hand on his chest, and kissed him. For a long moment she stood there, pressed against him, then she pulled back and shuddered slightly. "Don't die. I'm getting the exclusive from you on this."

"And we have that other thing to settle."

"If you make it through this, there'll be a different kind of 'thing' to settle." She smiled.

Ravenwood gently pushed her towards the door. He stood up straight and said, "Anyone who wants to quit, do it now."

Professor Johnny laughed. "It's just getting interesting."

"I go where he goes," Nathan added.

"Alright then, gentlemen, let's do it."

He started for the wooden door that led underground.

Ravenwood was unsteady as he descended the circular stairs. He wished for more light, for a better idea than to go chasing into the tunnels, looking for a crazy scientist bent on breaking the back of a city by causing it terrible hallucinations and inducing rage in everyone.

And yet, here he was. He shook his head as he got to the bottom, and looked around. The tunnel before him was as narrow as the stairs had been, but at least he had room to stand up. Every five or six feet was an indentation for an upright crypt. He hefted his Luger and picked up the lit torch in front of him on the wall.

Professor Johnny and Nathan had brought along flashlights.

Ravenwood hugged the right wall, moving swiftly down the corridor.

"What are we looking for, exactly?" the professor whispered.

"I think we'll know it when we see it."

They came to the end of the initial corridor. It went left and right, and for a moment, Ravenwood had no idea which way to go. Except that down here, with limited air, the torch would be drawn to the source of the air.

It was being drawn to the left. He gestured, and they turned. He moved slower here, as he figured that the source of the air flowing in would actually be the place where the scientist, and possibly Maria would be.

The corridor began to narrow, with the walls tapering to a point. Another dozen feet on, it was so narrow that Ravenwood had to walk with his back to one side, the torch behind him, and his pistol in front of him. He didn't want to lead with the torch because he couldn't defend himself with it as efficiently as with the pistol.

The squeeze began another three steps later, when he noted the difficulty he had in drawing a full breath. Panic began to eat at the back of his mind as a feeling of asphyxiation set in around him. He tried to move more quickly, but the walls were slowing him down too much. Two more steps, and he wasn't sure he could go any further.

He could see that another three feet away was a right angle that opened up into a broader tunnel. He just had to squeeze.

He shoved through, and sucked in a huge gust of air. Over his labored breathing, he could hear water flowing.

"I think we found them."

"Put your torch out," Professor Johnny advised. There was enough ambient light before the trio to proceed without either the torch or their flashlights.

They moved forward, now cloaked in meager shadows. The closer they got to the entrance to the underground water system, the more Ravenwood could hear the commotion of someone moving something quite large. He put his back to the wall, raised his Luger, and rounded the corner, cloaked in darkness.

There was a whole laboratory set-up on the farthest side of the channel, with a metal bridge connecting the two sides with water dividing. Also on the farthest side was a huge beaker of a gray liquid swirling ominously in its container, and a tube running down from the beaker to the water supply. Mrs. Abrams was working feverishly at one end of the laboratory set-up while another man in a white coat was working on the opposite side.

There was a uniformed police officer looking on from the metal bridge.

The white lab-coat suddenly stopped, and looked up. "We're not alone, Officer Barlow."

The cop wheeled, drawing his service revolver. It was the same cop from the cemetery, the one whose aura reeked of evil and rage. Now Ravenwood knew why.

"Drop your weapons!" Officer Barlow roared.

"Not gonna happen." Ravenwood leveled the pistol at the cop.

"I wasn't asking."

Ravenwood sensed Nathan next to him, knew that the young man could kill the corrupt cop without anyone else getting hurt. Ravenwood wondered if he could be disarmed, instead. He looked around quickly, sensing what he could of the room. His power couldn't touch anything beyond the bridge, and knew that someone, either the man in the white lab coat or the officer was blocking him somehow.

Ravenwood tightened his grip on the walking stick and began whispering quietly. He found some energy that wasn't tainted by the evil so close to him, and summoned it. The power expanded slowly inside him as he drew it to him. He lifted the walking stick very slowly, less than two inches off the ground, channeled the power, and stabbed the stick into the concrete.

A wave of blue light erupted from the end of the staff and blew outward in a roiling mass. The cop was thrown backwards, down onto the bridge. Nathan took off at a sprint to disarm the officer. Ravenwood's power slammed into a barrier around the lab. The energy shimmered around the barrier, off around the corners of the concrete walls, into the side tunnels.

Ravenwood thought he spotted something.

The man in the white coat beside Mrs. Abrams turned slowly, and smiled.

"Impressive, isn't it?"

"One of the beautiful things about alchemy," Maria Abrams said proudly. "Science, coupled with magic allows us to conjure such forces that you can't even fathom."

"She's not wrong." Ravenwood recognized him instantly as the man in the photographs with Monica. It was Andrew, her boyfriend the chemist.

"Why?" Professor Johnny asked.

"Because it's time to change things," Andrew said, approaching a metallic handle that would release the toxin into the water-supply for New York City, where it'd spread like wildfire and contaminate city, and any point west that the water flowed to.

Nathan was crouched next to the cop, taking away the man's pistol and baton. He tightened his grip on the weighted metal stick.

"We'll stop you," Ravenwood said.

"No you won't," Andrew retorted.

"You have to disable the field for the toxin to escape."

The man's eyes flashed for a moment as Ravenwood realized he was seeing through the façade. There was no magic here, only science. His police friends often remarked that the best crimes that took months, even years to plan were usually the easiest to solve. There was always a trail to follow. It was the "spur of the moment" crimes that haunted good cops. Mrs. Abrams didn't seem to notice.

"It's not just a simple toxin," Maria elaborated. "It's an elixir from our gods."

"Uh-huh," Ravenwood nodded. "Go ahead, throw the switch."

"Are you mad?" Professor Johnny hissed.

"Look around, Professor."

Professor Johnny adjusted the grip on his weapon, and casually walked over to the left. While he moved, Nathan stood up slowly.

"Do it, Andrew," Maria commanded. "Show them."

There was a central machine, set away from the lab table, with heavy black cables running away from it to the left and right, around the corners. Ravenwood looked at it, saw the gleaming nickel-plated spheres on top, and it began to dawn on him.

"Drop the weapons!" A woman's voice snapped behind them. Ravenwood guessed it was Monica Abrams.

"You look good for a corpse," he commented wryly.

"My blood was the catalyst for our gods."

"Uh-huh," he looked back at the lab. "Was it your idea or your boy-friend's to fake your death and begin this little project?"

"Ours together," she said smugly in a voice that sounded like bells ringing.

"Very impressive," Ravenwood confessed. "It has all worked out so wonderfully."

"She said put your weapons down!" Andrew said with rage creeping into his voice.

"No," Ravenwood replied calmly.

"Do it, now."

"No," Ravenwood repeated.

He looked to the left; saw the professor with one hand resting comfortably in his pocket while the other held a pistol on Monica. Ravenwood kept his pistol aimed at Andrew, while Nathan also aimed at the alchemist.

"This ends now." Andrew lunged for the machine and heaved the switch. Immediately, liquid began to flow from the huge storage beakers, down the tubes towards the water. He turned, and began to run. Nathan shoved off in a sprint after him.

Ravenwood twisted around and slammed his walking stick into Monica's gun. It went flying away and he kicked her in the chest, sending her down hard. Professor Johnny hauled something from his pocket and lobbed it into the water.

"Get away from there!" The professor yelled at Nathan as the assistant careened head-long into the barrier. Electricity shimmered as he hit it, and was thrown backwards with such force that he landed brutally on his back next to Ravenwood.

The object that Professor Johnny threw exploded, and white lighting erupted up into the barrier, causing it to flash and tremble until it reached the sources, and exploded. Andrew's eyes widened in horror, and he wheeled to run.

Ravenwood raced after him. Andrew rounded the corner to the right, and Ravenwood fired a shot at him. It went wide, hit the concrete wall. Andrew flinched, and kept running. He stole a glance backwards and saw Nathan staggering across the bridge to deactivate the machine. Maria was screaming, trying to keep Ravenwood and his friends away from the device.

When he rounded the corner, he saw the giant electromagnetic coil with a generator coil down in the water, drawing hydroelectric power from the flow of the water. He raced past it, and fired another shot at Andrew. This one grazed him on the side, and he yelled. Andrew staggered a couple of steps, then threw himself around another corner.

With the barrier down, Ravenwood had his foresight back, so when he reached the corner he dove head-long across the gap, into cover, while Andrew fired off two shots from his .45 caliber pistol. The hand-gun boomed like thunder in the narrow confines. Ravenwood glanced around the corner and saw Andrew run away.

"You can't stop this!" Andrew shouted as he got to the bottom of the ladder. Ravenwood fired down two more shots, and heard Andrew scream after the second one. He stepped into the tube and slid to the bottom. Once there, he looked around rapidly. There was a pool of blood on the floor, and drops leading away. Ravenwood followed them quickly, surprised by the labyrinth of tunnels beneath the water network above him.

Ravenwood reloaded the Luger, and moved quickly. He wouldn't be surprised by his foe in these tunnels. No person could spook Ravenwood when he could foresee that person's movement.

He rounded a corner and he heard a metallic click as something activated. He twisted and threw himself down as the explosion ripped through the air where his torso had just been. Debris and pebbles landed across him as the dust fell. Pain stabbed at his brain from where the jagged rocks gouged his wounded arms.

He sensed Andrew coming, but his mind was foggy. He tried to lift the pistol, found he was too stunned to do so. The explosion had rendered his body useless with shock. He looked up slowly as Andrew appeared, pistol raised.

A clarity settled over his mind that he couldn't fathom. He found the ability to lift the Luger, and yelled, "Stop!" but it wasn't Ravenwood's voice, it was the Nameless One's.

Andrew kept coming. "I have to do this!" he held a smaller vial of the toxin in his hand, and the .45 in the other. "I have to see this through!"

Andrew aimed the pistol to fire, but Ravenwood's Luger went off first. He fired two shots to the alchemist's chest, and he staggered backward, the spasm making him fire off one round into the concrete wall. He hit the ground hard, and lay still. The vial was intact when his last breath escaped him.

Ravenwood staggered to his feet, and lurched for the ladder to climb back to the surface.

❋ ❋ ❋

Both Maria Abrams and her daughter Monica were arrested alive and relatively unharmed. They both believed whole-heartedly that they were doing the will of an ancient alchemist god. They were both sadly misled. They would have time in prison to think it through.

Nathan had managed to subdue the dirty cop without killing him, and thus eliminated the need to explain that to Inspector Stagg. Lilly had brought the detective and his squad right as everything was being wrapped up under the church. Professor Johnny's electric explosion had also caused the deployment tubes of the toxin to melt shut, and prevented the escape of any of the toxin into New York's water supply.

Inspector Stagg didn't believe any of it, he still was skeptical even after Ravenwood gave him a tour of the underground facility. It didn't matter, however, because it was over and finished.

As for the original case that Ravenwood had been hired to solve, it was quite simple. The old man who had been disturbed in his final sleep was actually the architect of the entire scheme. He was the fellow who had come up with the electromagnets that had protected the laboratory from ambush or detection. It was a smaller version of the same device that distorted Ravenwood's vision inside that house at the beginning. Mrs. Langston was a hesitant participant. She believed that the electromagnets were just a way to remain hidden while they did their alchemist's work.

All and all, it had been a really long day. Even though Ravenwood didn't need much sleep, found it a waste of time, he was bone tired when things were done that day. He was on his way when he discovered that Stagg had brought along Ravenwood's Ford as a 'thank-you' from the department. They had footed the bill for the repairs.

He collapsed ungracefully inside the Ford's driver's seat and fired it up. He was letting the engine warm up when Lilly climbed into the passenger seat.

"Go away."

"Nope."

"I mean it."

"So do I. You owe me an exclusive, remember? You get to deliver it now." She looked at the backs of his arms, "And I can take care of that."

He looked at her, ran his eyes up her slender body, and smiled.

"Maybe in the morning."

"Drinks and business first. Then we can, uh, sort things out," she smiled coyly.

He put the car in gear, and pulled away from the curb. Maybe the night wouldn't be a total loss after all.

The End

WRITING RAVENWOOD

The primary idea for this story came out of a video game I was playing at the time. John Dee and alchemy was referenced for about two minutes, and then the plot moved on. But I was fascinated by the idea of alchemy, so I got to studying, and found a metric ton of interesting things.

So when I was offered the opportunity to write Ravenwood, Stepson of Mystery, I realized this alchemy research I'd been doing was perfect for the story. I built the idea around it, and went to town.

Ravenwood himself is an interesting fellow. The idea of a rich, bored playboy who investigates the weird and the supernatural because of his own strange abilities is very, very cool.

One challenge for me came in the writing of suspense. It's not usually that difficult to fathom, but when a character can accurately predict the next few moments of action, how do you build suspense when the hero already knows what's going to happen? The solution turned out to be fairly simple.

Create circumstances where that ability is useless or ineffective. In turn, that became great fun. Constructing the world around Ravenwood proved to be an interesting character study. It gave me a unique opportunity to set up Ravenwood's unique abilities, the characters he interacts with, and the world he exists in, all without breaking narrative flow.

When I started with Airship 27, I was offered several different assignments with a variety of characters. I chose Ravenwood because he seemed like the most interesting and most straightforward character to write about.

The really difficult part in creating the story was finding Ravenwood's voice. He's been written about by a variety of authors, so finding my own perspective on the Man of Mystery was a tricky bit of fictional voodoo.

Ravenwood was a great character to write about. Creating his story was energizing and exciting, and I am hugely grateful for the opportunity to step into such interesting fictional shoes.

JONATHAN FISHER – is a Professional Rally Novelist. He specializes in action/adventure, suspense, horror, thriller, mystery and science fiction. He started writing seriously at age 13, when his grandmother gave him a portable Underwood typewriter, manufactured in 1912. He has been writing eagerly ever since.

He has an active Tumblr account discussing the literary and gaming universe, at thejollywriter.tumblr.com.

"HEART OF DARKNESS"

by Gene Moyers

Driving conditions were terrible. It was almost dark. Large drops of rain were starting to pound the ground. The wind was blowing and the intervals between the flash of lightning and the rumble of the following thunder were shrinking fast. Jack Cordona was late getting back to the warehouse. The rain had slowed his afternoon deliveries. It was going to be a wet night and he didn't look forward to waiting for his bus home. A flash of lightning lit the cab of the large stake bed truck and the following boom of thunder followed less than a second behind. Getting closer, he thought as he gripped the steering wheel more tightly. The wind whipped a burst of heavy rain onto the windshield and the wipers fought to keep the glass clean. Jack peered through the rain splatters and could see the headlights of two oncoming cars between weak sweeps of the wipers.

As the cars neared there was a huge flash and a jagged bolt of lightning flashed down to strike a power pole at the right shoulder of the road. Jack didn't hear the crack of the wood as it shattered, but he could clearly see the pole falling into his path trailing wires in its wake. Instinctively, he swerved to the left. This threw him into the path of the first oncoming car. Jack swore and wrenched the wheel back to the right. He almost made it. The corner of his heavy bumper and left front fender scraped down the side of the Ford coupe throwing up bright sparks. The sideswiped coupe swerved and ran off the shoulder and down the bank. Jack didn't see this as he madly stabbed the brakes with both feet. The wheels failed to grip the soaked roadway and he slammed nearly head-on into the following sedan.

For a moment Jack sat behind the wheel stunned. He had banged his forehead on the steering wheel but otherwise seemed unharmed; the truck's large bulk had saved him from serious injury. What of the other cars? He shouldered the driver's door open, jumped to the ground and made his way forward. The sedan was pinned under the truck's front bumper. Steam spiraled up from under the crumpled hood. Jack made his way to the passenger side window. Cupping his hands around his eyes he leaned into window and peered through the glass. The window was slightly opaque from condensation, but he could make out the shape of a single figure behind the wheel. The driver was unmoving, his arms hanging down at his sides and head resting on the steering wheel. As Jack wrenched open the car door, a flash of lightning revealed a one-storied building across the road with cars parked in front of it. He could see several figures with flashlights running toward the wreck. In the light of the headlights of a car that had pulled up behind the sedan, Jack leaned in and grasped the driver's right hand. He thought he detected a pulse. There were people crowding in behind him others attempting to open the driver's door. Voices clamored, "Anybody hurt?" "What happened?" Jack backed out of the car and raised his voice, "Any doctors here? This man's hurt."

A man shouldered him aside."Let me take a look."

Jack turned. "What about the other car. Is the driver okay?"

Someone said, "What other car?"

Jack looked around. He didn't see the other car at all through the driving rain. He walked up the shoulder of the road. As he passed the rear of the truck, he saw a glow from down the bank through the bushes. Cupping his hands, he shouted, "Hey, over here. We need some help!" He pushed down the bank and through a screen of bushes, skidded on some mud and wound up in waist deep, cold water. A few yards ahead he could see the other car. It was resting rear first in the swollen creek mostly submerged with only the hood, front wheels and top of roof visible.

Jack waded forward and pulled on the driver's door, but the force of the water rushing past held it closed. In seconds he had half dozen hands assisting him. Their combined strength managed to tear it open. Inside the driver lay slumped in the water that nearly filled the car's interior. Within seconds, the rescuers had him out of the car and were attempting to pull him up the bank. It was not easy manhandling the limp body up the muddy bank, and the rescuers slipped and cursed on the muddy slope, but soon they had him lying face up on the shoulder of the road.

Jack put his ear to the driver's chest. He listened a few seconds and sat up. He looked up at the surrounding faces. "He isn't breathing." Another man knelt down and grabbed the driver. "Here, help me turn him on his side." Willing hands quickly helped turned him. Another man pulled his hands over his head while a third began pushing on his side and back. Jack watched the attempts to revive him and thought they were probably useless but he held his tongue. He was therefore totally surprised when just as the scene was illuminated by another flash of lightning the driver vomited up an obscene amount of water and gasped. A ragged cheer went up as the man coughed, gasped, spit up more water and began coughing almost continuously. Men gently turned him face up and Jack got his first really good look at the man they had rescued. He was middle aged, going bald on top, and looked exactly as Jack would picture a bookkeeper. But he was going to make it and Jack drew a sigh of relief. He heard rapid steps behind him and a voice at his shoulder, "Say, is this guy okay?"

A man holding the driver's hand looked up and smiled. "Yeah, I think he's going to make it."

The man at Jack's shoulder answered, "That's good, because the other guy just died."

Jack turned to look, first at the speaker and then down the road to toward the sedan, now illuminated by several flashlights and lanterns. He could hear approaching sirens as the rain continued to beat down.

✳ ✳ ✳

"Thank you, Sterling," Ravenwood smiled at his manservant as he handed over his hat, overcoat, gloves and his companion's wrap.

"How was the symphony sir? Stimulating?"

"Wonderful Sterling, I always enjoy Beethoven."

Sterling nodded and asked, "May I bring you and the lady some champagne?"

"No, thank you, Sterling, I'll see to our needs." He turned to follow the elegantly dressed young lady through the double doors into his study. He entered and closed the doors behind him, "Would you like a brandy, Sophia?"

The attractive woman gave him a smile that lit up the room and answered, "That would be lovely."

As he poured a fine cognac from a cut crystal decanter into to oversized snifters, Ravenwood subtly watched his companion. Sophia Scoggins was certainly worth looking at. Medium height, brunette, brown eyes with a full figure that certainly did justice to the baby blue evening dress she wore. He crossed the room and handed her the glass. "Thank you, Ravenwood. My, that is so formal, when are you going to tell me your first name?'

Ravenwood touched the rim of his snifter against hers and listened to the clear ring the leaded crystal made as he smiled. "Darling, you know I don't have a first name. My parents were far too poor to afford one."

Sophia threw her head back and laughed. "You have the strangest sense of humor."

He moved to the tall French doors, threw them wide and stepped out onto the balcony. The fall night was pleasantly cool. Recent heavy thunderstorms had brought cooling relief from the warm humid weather they had been having lately. He sipped and looked out over the lights of the city. Sophia glided out behind him and stood close enough to him that he could smell her expensive perfume. She sighed, "What a lovely view. I love the estate but sometimes I wish my family would move into the city. Perhaps I should take an apartment by myself." She glanced slyly at him and said, "We could see more of each other then."

Ravenwood was spared the necessity of replying by Sterling's voice. "I beg your pardon sir, but there is a representative of. . . "

Ravenwood spoke, "The police. Yes, show him in."

Sterling nodded and withdrew.

Ravenwood bowed slightly to Sophia, "Excuse me, I'll just be a moment." He then followed Sterling to the entry hall. A uniformed patrolman stood by the door, hat in hand. As Ravenwood neared he stiffened into semi-attention. "Mr. Ravenwood, sir."

Glancing at his nametag Ravenwood asked, "What can I do for you, Officer Dunphy?"

"Well sir, Detective Selfridge sent me to fetch you, er, uh, I mean to ask you if you could come down right away to the Sellwood Apartments, sir."

Ravenwood's chameleon-like eyes darkened. "Indeed and why would my presence be necessary?"

"Well, sure an' there's been a terrible crime, sir, a murder," he dropped his voice at the last.

Ravenwood nodded and took a sip of cognac. He raised his voice, "Sterling!" He turned and Sterling was advancing toward him, his hat and gloves in one hand, his walking stick in the other and his overcoat over one arm. Ravenwood nodded and quickly exchanged his glass for his outdoor clothing. Once in his coat and hat he moved quickly to Sophia, who had followed into the hallway.

"I'm very sorry, my dear, but I'm afraid I must leave. The police apparently have a little problem they need my advice on. Please forgive me for rushing off."

Sophia looked at him wonderingly. "You did say you were an amateur detective of sorts. Does this happen often?"

He smiled. "More often than I like." He leaned in and kissed her lightly on the cheek, getting a good whiff of that perfume. "Sterling, call Miss Scoggins a cab."

"Of course, sir."

He smiled. "I'll call you tomorrow about dinner." He slipped on his gloves. "Lead on, officer." He turned and waved to Sophia as he followed the officer out the front door. She waved gently back.

Use of the siren made short work of the journey across town. As they pulled up in front of an expensive apartment building, Ravenwood mused about getting a similar siren for his roadster, totally illegal of course. He was smiling as the front door was opened by a uniformed officer. The doorman was nowhere in sight. They took the elevator to the ninth floor. When the doors opened, Ravenwood could see another officer standing outside an apartment door. Once in the apartment, he saw one officer taking multiple photos of the living room and another one dusting for fingerprints. More voices came from the kitchen. Dunphy cleared his throat and said unnecessarily, "They'd be waiting for you in the kitchen, sir."

Nodding, Ravenwood stepped across the threshold. As he did he immediately felt it, a sense of death and . . .evil. He glanced around as he walked across the living room. His eyesight had that ultra-clearness he had grown accustomed to when his senses were aroused. Near the kitchen door he looked down, the carpet had a shimmery aura to it in a trail leading back the way he had come ending near the front door. He nodded to himself and entered the kitchen. A plainclothes detective was leaning against the counter writing in a notebook. Detective Selfridge was kneeling on the floor next to the body. He looked up, rose to his feet and stepped forward hand extended, "Mr. Ravenwood, thank you for coming. I appreciate it."

Shaking the detective's hand he said, "Not at all Detective. It's a pleasure to meet you again. I'm sorry it is under these circumstances." He had met the young detective a few months before, and had found him bright and dedicated, but also practical and open to Ravenwood's sometimes unusual conclusions. "What do we have?"

"Well, sir, this apparently is one Kenneth Larsen, age forty-two, a successful real estate agent. He was last seen yesterday leaving his office about four o'clock. He was found earlier this evening by the apartment manager. As you can see, it is quite unusual." He waved a vague hand at the body.

Ravenwood squatted down next to the body. Larsen, a medium-built man, was lying on his back, arms at his side, naked from the waist up. Ravenwood's eyes were immediately drawn to the victim's chest. His chest had been cut open in a long vertical incision. The edges of the incision had been pulled back and ribs pried out of the way. Leaning forward, he could clearly see that the victim's heart was missing. Tearing his eyes away from the gaping chest wound, he quickly noted the deep purple bruising around Larsen's neck, his face was also purple and his swollen tongue protruded slightly, from his parted lips. He had been strangled. Ravenwood moved slightly peering closely at the victim's hands, the wound on his chest and then his head. He turned it to one side and examined that back of the head. His grey eyes darkened and he stood up and motioned to the detective. "Look at the back of the head."

Selfridge squatted down and felt around the head. "There's a bump, a good sized one, but no broken skin."

Ravenwood agreed, "Not serious enough to kill him, but probably enough to stun for a short time."

Reentering the living room, he closed his eyes, took a breath and when he opened them his grey eyes had darkened to blue in concentration. Again he could see the shimmery aura along the carpet. Getting down on his knees, he examined the carpet closely. He seemed to see a path of shimmering energy. He followed it to the front door. Getting down once more, he could see a psychic imprint of where a body had been face down in the pattern of the carpet. This psychic trail would be invisible to any one not trained by the Nameless One.

Above him a sarcastic voice spoke, "Well if it isn't the poor man's Houdini. What are you doing at my crime scene and who called you anyway?"

Ravenwood stood up. Inspector Stagg hadn't changed any since the last time they had met. He was wearing the same rumpled suit and his hand in its side pocket was probably reaching for the bag of peanuts he was always munching on. As Ravenwood smiled at him he grimaced and turned his glare on the hapless Detective Selfridge. "Selfridge! Is this your doing?"

Selfridge wilted a little bit under Stagg's glare. "Well, Inspector, I thought considering the circumstances of the crime that Mr. Ravenwood could. . ."

"Yes, yes. Mr. Ravenwood could gaze into his crystal ball and tell us everything about who killed him." He swung his glare back to Ravenwood as if it were a police .38 lining up on his head. "Well Mesmer, what do the stars tell you?"

Ravenwood continued to smile. Stagg did not believe in anything he couldn't slap cuffs on. He hated it when Ravenwood's conclusions invariably were proven true and he really hated to accept his help. "Well, Inspector, I believe the victim went to the door, admitted his killer and when he turned his back on him, he was struck on the head." He pointed to the carpet in the hallway. "He was strangled here and then dragged into the kitchen where he was later undressed and his heart removed." Stagg looked skeptical. Ravenwood continued as he moved toward the kitchen and pointed at the corpse, "The killer had some knowledge of biology and used very sharp implements, possibly medical type equipment."

When he finished, he looked placidly at the inspector. Stagg sneered and sarcastically replied, "Oh, the killer was a doctor making a house call and then changed his mind and cut out his patient's heart. Are the Med schools short of cadavers to train on? Where do you come up with these things, Ravenwood? And what makes you such an expert on body mutilation?"

Ravenwood replied mildly, "What is your explanation, Inspector?"

"Well, it's obvious. The killer is insane, probably with a record of psychological illness. He surely has some kind of 'Jack the Ripper' fantasy of killing and taking body parts as trophies," he smiled triumphantly.

Ravenwood smiled back. "Well, Inspector, I'm sure you're probably correct. It's late, and I must go. Could I trouble you for a ride?"

"Anything to get you out of my hair." He waved a hand at a patrolman. "Peterson, take this guy anywhere he wants to go." As Ravenwood followed the patrolman to the door, he stopped and turned back toward Stagg. "He's going to kill again, and he won't be taking a liver next time. He wants the hearts for something, something important." Stagg just glared at him as he left the apartment.

In the back of the squad car, Ravenwood was silent as his thoughts reached out. A voice came to his mind. "You are correct. This murder was evil. The killer has purpose. The heart is a powerful symbol. It can be used in fearful rituals. This killer will kill again." Upon reaching Sussex Towers, he thanked the policeman, entered the building and took the express elevator to his thirtieth floor penthouse where he retired for the night.

Ravenwood spent the next morning doing some research in his library and then consulted the phone book. After lunch, he gathered up his hat and gloves. He made a quick stop in the kitchen to tell Sterling he probably would eat out for dinner before he powered away in his roadster headed downtown. It was easy to find Larsen's real estate office in the Macon building. As he entered, a young girl was speaking on the telephone. Her eyes looked swollen. She was explaining to a client that Mr. Larsen had been killed and the office was closed. When she hung up she wiped her nose with tissue and looked at Ravenwood, "You heard that Mr. Larsen died yesterday." He nodded. "Then you understand the office is closed."

Ravenwood looked directly at her. Pitching his voice low to attune with her emotions he spoke. "You are Larsen's secretary." She nodded. He continued speaking carefully, asking her if Larsen had any enemies or if anyone had made threats against him. She responded that Larsen had a few unhappy clients, one in particular had been calling lately, a Professor Hartley. Ravenwood asked her if she had eaten lunch. When she replied that she wasn't hungry he told her that she was very hungry. He told her to go to lunch and return in one hour. Further he told her to lock the office after her. Lastly, he told her she would not remember him or his visit.

Silently, the girl gathered purse and hat and left the office. Seeing no file cabinets, he moved to the door to the inner office marked private. It was locked. Placing his hand over the door atop the keyhole, he took a deep breath and summoned his powers. His hand tingling, he twisted it suddenly to the right and heard the door bolt click back.

Entering the office, he closed the door and leaned against it. It seemed like an ordinary office; file cabinets, a large desk, comfortable visitor's chairs and a sofa along one wall. Ravenwood closed his now dark eyes, took a breath and opened them. Slowly he scanned the room. The Rolodex on Larsen's desk seemed to have a glowing aura about it. His eyes moved on. The second drawer on the third file cabinet seemed to have a similar aura. He moved to the Rolodex and began flipping through it. A card seemed to glow: John Degraaf; with an address and two telephone numbers for home and office. Ravenwood pocketed it. Further flipping resulted in a second card with a glowing aura. This one was in the name of an Anthony Lorenzo, also with an address but only one phone number. Pocketing this also, he moved to the file cabinet. Opening the glowing drawer, he sorted through the client files. Finally, Ravenwood came to the file for a Stephen Hartley, a professor at the university. He was apparently an investor in some commercial property. The investment had not done very well. In fact, it looked like Hartley had lost quite a sum of money on this particular investment. Most interestingly, John Degraaf was listed as involved as well as "other" not listed investors. After noting Hartley's address and phone number, Ravenwood replaced the file. He then quietly left the office, locking the outer door after him. Having never removed his leather gloves, he didn't worry about fingerprints and the girl should have no memories of his visit.

Back at the Sussex he parked his car and started up the front steps but instead was drawn to the park across the street. He strolled through the park enjoying the leaves that were beginning to take on fall colors. He came to a small clearing covered in grass. The Nameless One was sitting cross-legged on the grass, his hands at his sides, his eyes closed. Silently, Ravenwood took a seat on a nearby bench.

Minutes passed before the old man spoke. "I sense that the boundary between this world and the netherworld is weakened. If it is pierced, there will be chaos. There will be more death if you cannot stop this evil."

Ravenwood nodded, "I know. I have an idea who may be behind this, and I may be able to save the next victim, but I do not know what is behind it all."

Without opening his eyes, the old man said, "This man intends to perform some dark ritual to gain power. Blood is power, and the taking of human hearts could bring a man much power if he has knowledge of the dark arts." Ravenwood waited but the old man did not speak again. After a few minute he quietly left.

Later, in his study, he was reading up on occult rituals when the telephone rang. Soon there was a discreet knock at the study door. Sterling entered. "Sorry sir, but there is a telephone call for you from the University." Ravenwood nodded and picked up the extension on his desk. It was the university calling to confirm his lecture tomorrow at one pm. He assured them of his presence. Hanging up, he remembered his promise to call Sophia. After a brief chat, she agreed to have dinner with him the day after tomorrow.

He continued studying until dark, then going to his bedroom, he changed his well-tailored suit for loose fitting black slacks and a long sleeve black shirt. Over this went his shoulder holster and Luger. To conceal this he then put on a light-weight cotton wind breaker. Taking up his leather gloves, he quietly left the penthouse. A few minutes later he was in his roadster, powering through the night.

He drove to the address of John DeGraaf. He saw no lights as he cruised past the well kept brownstone. He circled the block and parked down the street. He wanted to talk to DeGraaf about his dealings with Larsen, especially their land scheme with Professor Hartley. However, if he wasn't home, perhaps it might be better to go directly to the source. He started the roadster and headed for Hartley's house.

He had the address but it took a while to find Professor Hartley's house. It was just out of town in an area of small farms and large old family homes. The house was a large rambling Victorian with covered porches on all sides and a three-story turret. In the dim light he even thought he could discern a widow's walk on the steep roof. He parked some way down the road, and taking a flashlight from the glove box he walked back to the house keeping to the deep shadows under the large trees.

The house was set on a large piece of ground, and there were no houses

"There will be more death if you cannot stop this evil."

closer than a quarter mile. No lights showed in the house. Ravenwood waited quietly under the tree until he was satisfied that the house was empty, and then he quietly approached. He thought about it and decided to try the back door. Concentrating his mind, he moved his hand sharply across the door, unlocking it. Using the flashlight sparingly, he found himself in a small entryway. Through a doorway was a large kitchen. To his right was a narrow stairway going up, to his left a closed door and ahead was an open doorway to the dining room. He tried the door to his left. It opened inward and exposed steep stairs going downward into blackness. The hairs on the back of Ravenwood's neck rose gently. Evil emanated from the darkness as does cold air from an open window. He hesitated and then closed the door. It was here he needed to explore but the rest of the house must come first.

He made a quick tour of the ground floor: dining room, parlor, library, an unused sewing room, all were empty. Ravenwood swept his light beam over the books in a cursory examination. There were some books of fiction, quite a few books on history as well as a scattering of other non-fiction subjects. Upstairs he carefully checked the bedrooms. Two were unused, with beds stripped of bedding. A small one showed occupancy. Personal items and a few books were scattered about. The closet contained normal clothing and several semi-formal suits of simple cut, apparently a butler's working clothes.

Ravenwood struck gold with the next room. A large bedroom over-looking the front of the house had been converted into a study. He drew the heavy drapes to hide his light while he searched. A large desk dominated the room while the right wall consisted solely of glass fronted cabinets containing many strange artifacts; to the left was a wall of bookshelves. Ravenwood could see many small statuettes, carvings, tools and native weapons behind the glass. These seemed to come from many native cultures. There were also more modern artifacts; a bell, what appeared to be a silver chalice, unusual mineral samples and various jars and bottles some with labels many without. Ravenwood could sense power here with hints of dark overtones. He moved to the wall of bookshelves. They were perhaps half full with books, piles of yellowed paper and what seemed to be a few scrolls. Sifting quickly through some of the papers he could see that most of them seemed to be old diaries and journals. Moving on to the books, he quickly discerned that most of them concerned ancient history, religion or occult studies. The books and papers all exuded feelings of power, and more than a few items seemed very dark to Ravenwood's touch.

Stepping back, he surveyed the room. Professor Hartley was researching much more than academic subjects. Anyone with this much accumulated arcane knowledge had to be up to no good. It would be likely that such studies would lead him to the darkest rituals, the kind of rituals that might require the use of human sacrifice.

Grimly, Ravenwood left the study. He opened the door of the last room knowing what he would find. It contained a nicely appointed bedroom with a large canopied bed. A book on the nightstand about Roman history confirmed this as the Professor's bedroom. He wasted little time searching here. Everything interesting would be found in the study or the dark basement.

Back in the kitchen, he drew his Luger and started down the steps, his flashlight leading the way. Surprisingly, he went down more than twenty steps, very deep for a normal basement. He was disappointed when he reached the bottom of the stairs. Flashing his light around revealed a normal basement. An old,unused boiler stood in a corner. Various garden implements hung on the walls or stood in a corner. Boxes were piled along one wall. But there was a door in the opposite wall and the sense of evil seemed even stronger to Ravenwood as he crossed the basement to the solid locked door.

A bit of concentration and Ravenwood's mental strength quickly manipulated the lock. It swung toward him on well-oiled hinges. A doorway opened into a large room. It had a high vaulted ceiling and brick walls. Ravenwood's light showed tall, free-standing candelabras and three legged braziers probably use for illumination. In the center of the room there was a large circle painted on the floor, and in the circle a table. On the table was a shallow metal bowl. Examining it revealed ashes in the bottom. This was undoubtedly where Hartley performed his rituals. Ravenwood could feel the power here. Unbidden words formed in his mind: "You are correct. This man seeks great power. Here, the walls of reality are very thin. With the correct sacrifice, that reality can be breached. This is what is planned."

He set the bowl back and flashed his light along the walls. In a far corner something caught his eye. It turned out to be a small, heavily rusted locked metal door. This lock took some concentration; it had obviously not been opened for a long time. It took a great effort to finally force the old lock open with his mind. Setting the flashlight on the floor, he braced his foot against the wall and heaved backward. He was rewarded with a grinding movement. A second mighty effort and the door swung inward with a grinding screech of metal. Thrusting his light through the low doorway he saw a rough, low passage stretching away beyond the range of his light. He took a few steps in. The walls were of very rough stone while the floor was roughly paved with large stones, bare mud squeezing up between them. Roots reached down between the heavy overhead wooden beams. Ravenwood continued down the passageway for nearly a hundred steps before it ended in rough stone steps leading upward. When he raised the light it revealed a metal door overhead. The only lock seemed to be a large rusted bolt. This yielded to a few well-placed blows with the flashlight, but even with his shoulder braced against it, the stubborn door would not lift.

Ravenwood turned and made his way quickly back to the vaulted basement room. He swung the metal door back and forth a few times. It moved far easier but still screeched metal on metal. He was about to lock it with his mind when he heard, "Danger is near. Someone comes." Ravenwood moved quickly back through the basement toward the stairs.

Ravenwood took the basement steps two at a time. When he reached the top he stopped to listen. A key was turning in a lock and a door opening. Not ready for a confrontation, he quietly closed the basement door and eased his way toward the back door. Suddenly he stopped and cursed silently. He had forgotten to open the drapes in the study. Hartley was up to no good here, but he must be given no cause for alarm while more evidence of murder was located. He crossed to the back stairs as a light came on in the front of the house. Climbing the stairs silently he moved to the study. More lights were now on down stairs. In the study, he opened the drapes and slipped out into the hall once more. As he moved toward the back stairs, a light came on in the kitchen below. He turned and slipped into the nearest door. Closing it quietly, he found himself in one of the vacant bedrooms. In the dim light he moved to the window. Unlatching it, he raised the sash and looked down. It was at least a fifteen-foot drop to the ground. To his left there was nothing but smooth wall but to his right there was a drain pipe near the corner. Holstering the Luger, he tucked the flashlight into a pocket of the windbreaker and swung his leg over the window sill. Careful of his balance, he maneuvered all of his body out the window and managed to grab hold of the drain pipe. He reached back carefully and pushed the window down until it was closed. He froze for a moment listening, but all he could hear was soft music coming from somewhere in the house.

Reassured, Ravenwood slowly slipped down the drain pipe until he was four feet up and then dropped quietly to the ground. Again he paused for a few seconds but heard nothing out of place. Silently, he moved across the darkened yard and into the trees. He watched for a few minutes longer and caught a glimpse of a figure moving through the kitchen and dining room. Turning to orient himself with the house and grounds, he finally decided the tunnel under the basement ended somewhere to the left and farther back from the road than the house, perhaps in some out building concealed in the trees. That was good to know. He returned to his car thinking of a long bath, some brandy and some serious planning.

❋ ❋ ❋

The next morning Ravenwood pondered an important decision. How was he to get information about Hartley to Inspector Stagg without arousing any more of Stagg's suspicions? Ravenwood was guilty of breaking and entering, twice, not to mention concealing evidence. Ravenwood had to tread lightly because if Stagg ever got wind of what he had been up to, he wouldn't hesitate to arrest him. Perhaps some subtle questions along with use of "the voice" might do it. He left these thoughts for later and went to dress for his lecture.

Splendid in formal clothes, Ravenwood drove the short distance to the university. He was a familiar figure on campus as a guest lecturer on the Far East. Today he was giving a lecture on Eastern teachings and the power of the mind to a small group of a few dozen professors, university administration and the ever present wealthy donors. Ravenwood spoke about his time in Asia. He talked of mind-over-matter discipline and gave examples of extreme feats performed by Yogis and mystics such as fire walking. He demonstrated some simple tricks and ended his lecture by "levitating" a vase off the table in front of him. He didn't actually lift it; instead he took the opportunity to practice his "voice." Pitching his voice just so, he convinced the whole room that the vase was slowly raising off the table. He kept up his soothing patter and fooled everyone in the room. His lecture was a hit and he was rewarded with a warm round of applause. Afterwards he took questions and then everyone mingled while partaking of the generous buffet lunch arrayed along one wall of the room.

While chatting with a professor, he was approached by an attractive but modestly dressed young woman carrying a book. Smiling, she extended the book toward him, "Mr. Ravenwood, would you be so kind as to autograph your book?" Ravenwood took the book of Eastern lore he had written the year before and flipped to the title page. "Of course, my dear. What is your name?"

"Marian."

"Well, I hope you enjoyed it." He quickly scribbled best wishes along with her name and handed it back to her, "Do you work here at the university?"

"Yes, I'm secretary to the head of the history department."

Interested, he casually inquired, "Really? Are you acquainted with Professor Hartley? I believe he teaches here."

"Why, yes, Professor Hartley teaches ancient history and history of religion, although he hasn't been here lately. He started on a six-month sabbatical last month."

Quickly ad-libbing he replied, "That's too bad. I had hoped to speak with him concerning Eastern religions. Do you know where he has gone?"

"I'm not sure where he is. I do know he said he was researching a major project."

Ravenwood smiled grimly to himself. Yes a major project in his dark basement. "Thank you for the information, Marian. If you are interested in Eastern mysticism, perhaps we can discuss it over lunch some time, if you'd like."

Marian positively beamed. "Oh, I would like that very much, Mr. Ravenwood. You can always reach me at the history department any time."

As the attractive blonde turned away, Ravenwood spotted the rather rumpled figure of Inspector Stagg loitering at the buffet table near the door. He was trying to look unobtrusive and doing a very poor job of it. His worn suit and tired raincoat made him highly visible against the backdrop of the well-dressed university crowd. Ravenwood strolled through the small crowd, exchanging pleasantries until neared Stagg. "I wasn't expecting you to attend today, Inspector. Enjoying the buffet? I believe they have some peanuts. . ."

Stagg opened his mouth to make a furious reply and then he glanced around and swallowed whatever venom he was about spew out. Instead he lowered his voice to a stage whisper, "You couldn't pay me to listen to your line of bushwah. I just need you to come with me. . .quietly."

Ravenwood raised an eyebrow. "Really, Inspector, am I being arrested?"

Stagg startled to boil again but held his temper as he lowered his voice even more. "No you're not under arrest, much as I'd like that." He hesitated. "There's been another murder, the same as Larsen."

Serious now, Ravenwood replied, "Of course, let me get my hat and coat."

In his roadster, Ravenwood followed Stagg across town to a street in an upscale neighborhood. He parked behind Stagg's car. A black and white cruiser was parked in front of a brownstone and a uniformed patrolman stood at the door. Following Stagg into the house, he once again found several officers and lab men taking photographs and dusting for prints. Stagg led him to the bathroom. The scene was similar to Larsen's kitchen. A man's semi-naked body lay on the floor face up. Again there was a gaping hole in his chest, his face swollen and purple. Suspecting he already knew the answer, he asked Stagg, "Who was he?"

Consulting a notebook he recited, "The victim is John DeGraaf, age, forty-four. Formerly a banker, he is now some kind of financier. The body was discovered early this morning by a family member. Our best guess is he was killed sometime late last night. The coroner will be able to tell for sure. Everything else seems the same as our first victim."

Ravenwood agreed, everything was the same, right down to the evil taint that remained about the house, He frowned at the body; events were moving faster than anticipated. He needed to get Stagg onto the right track. His thoughts were interrupted by Stagg's sarcastic voice, "Well Mr. Wizard. What do you think?"

"I think the same as I did before. This isn't any more random than the first killing. Whoever is doing this has a purpose. Perhaps revenge, perhaps some kind of ritual, but he has a plan and it's not finished yet. Is there any kind of connection between Larsen and this Degraaf?"

"Plan! What kind of maniac has a plan to cut people's hearts out? And no, we haven't found any connection. . .yet. I'm sending someone over to Larsen's office to go over his files."

"When I was there yesterday I spoke to the secretary and she. . ."

"What were you doing at Larsen's office?" Stagg squinted at him suspiciously.

"Just asking a few questions. She mentioned that Larsen had taken a few angry phone calls lately. She thinks it might have been one of his clients. If an angry client had lost a lot of money in a land scheme to Larsen, it might be that Degraaf was involved. That might be your connection."

Stagg just stared at him suspiciously. "Maybe we'll look into that." He then sneered,."Got any more revelations?"

Ravenwood shook his head. "No, I've seen enough. Let me know if you need any more help, Inspector." He walked briskly to the door. He felt a desperate need to get to this car. Once there, he fired up the big twelve-cylinder engine and screeched away from the curb. As he sped through the city streets, he mentally flayed himself. He had waited too long to save DeGraaf. He had to get to Lorenzo to warn him if it wasn't too late.

He couldn't wait for Stagg to find the connections between the three and Hartley.

His research on Lorenzo showed he lived on the outskirts of town in an upscale area of large estates. Upon reaching the proper address, he pulled up in the driveway and was confronted by a metal gate. The driveway curved fifty yards up to a large, two storied and modern mansion. A man in a plain cut suit stepped out of a small booth next to the gate. He swaggered over to the roadster. "This is private property. Beat it," he said, jerking a thumb toward the road.

Ravenwood inquired, "Does Anthony Lorenzo live here?"

The obvious hood eyed Ravenwood carefully. "Don't matter none who lives here. Beat it." He reached toward his hip, going for a gun or sap, Ravenwood was sure. Looking the guard in the eye he spoke with a vibrating tone, "Stop. Now tell me the truth."

The guard froze and slowly nodded. Ravenwood looked to the house. "Is Lorenzo at home?" The guard nodded. "Is he alright?" Another nod. He then proceeded to pump the helpless guard for information. Within minutes he learned that Anthony Lorenzo was a former bootlegger who still had underworld connections. He was wealthy and the guard thought "he had his fingers in a lot of pies." John DeGraaf was a frequent visitor to the Lorenzo estate. The guard had heard of Larsen but did not know him by sight. He wasn't privy to Lorenzo's private plans but he thought that Lorenzo, DeGraaf and Larsen were in business together. He had never heard of Professor Hartley.

Having learned everything he could from the addled guard, Ravenwood was about to leave when he noticed several men trotting toward the gate from the house. All were carrying weapons of some kind. Backing out onto the road, he stepped on the gas pedal and sped away from the estate. Ravenwood now knew that Larsen and DeGraaf, backed by Lorenzo's crooked money, were running land deals; some probably honest, some not. They had roped Hartley into one of these schemes and he had lost money, perhaps a lot of money. Unfortunately for Larsen and DeGraaf, they had chosen the wrong victim. Undoubtedly the history professor had been studying obscure texts and lore for many years. Somewhere along the way, he had stepped over the line and begun practicing the dark arts. Now, cheated of his money, he was taking his revenge and intended to use his victim's hearts to increase his power. Surely, his next intended victim was Lorenzo, but Lorenzo seemed well guarded. If Hartley couldn't get to Lorenzo, would he choose another victim? And would Lorenzo figure out who had killed his partners and what would he do? Ravenwood had to hope that Inspector Stagg would make the connection between Larsen, DeGraaf and Lorenzo soon, but would he figure Hartley's part in it? Perhaps. Still figuring how to help things along without giving himself away, he decided to go to Hartley's house and keep watch.

It was late afternoon and traffic was heavy. By the time Ravenwood reached Hartley's house it was nearly dark. He parked in an overgrown side road that might have been a driveway years before. He couldn't see anything so he got out and started through the woods toward Hartley's house. It occurred to him that he was somewhere in the neighborhood of the basement tunnel entrance. He stopped to orient himself and moved off in the gathering gloom, pushing through scattered brush and despairing of what his tailor would say about what he was doing to a perfectly good tuxedo. After fifty yards or so, Ravenwood could see a dim shape ahead. Focusing his eyes and reaching out with his senses, he could make out the ruins of a building. The remains of crumbling walls took shape. It was not a barn. More likely it had been a storage building or carriage house. He looked to his right and could make out lights about a hundred yards away through the trees. These ruins had to be where the underground passage from the basement led.

He turned and made his way toward the Hartley house. Brush soon thinned and he was forced to make his way from tree to tree. He stopped behind a large one thirty yards away and settled in to watch. There were lights in the kitchen and dining room but he could see no one. There were also lights in one room upstairs. He watched for nearly a half hour. During that time he saw an older man with glasses pass through to the kitchen and back again. He was casually dressed and carrying a newspaper. It was hard to tell from this quick glimpse, but Ravenwood got no feelings as this man passed in front of the windows. He didn't know exactly what Hartley looked like but he didn't think this man was him. But if it wasn't, who was he?

Keeping to the deep shadows beneath the trees, Ravenwood made his way around the house where he could see the front. There was a light on in the living room but the drapes were drawn. More interesting, there was a light on in Hartley's study. He settled in again. Time passed and he pulled his jacket closer about him. He was getting cold and was painfully aware that he had eaten only a few hors d'oeuvres since breakfast. He glanced at his watch. It was nearly 9 pm. He had just decided to get closer to the house when suddenly the upstairs study light went out. He waited, and within five minutes the front door opened. A man was silhouetted against the light. He paused and said something over his shoulder to someone unseen in the living room and closed the door. As he started down the front steps and across the lawn, Ravenwood turned and ran through the trees in the direction of his car. Trusting to his sense of danger and quick reflexes, he ran full speed. He was nearly there when a car passed him on the road. Fortunately, there were enough trees and brush between him and the road that he could not be seen. Reaching his roadster, he threw himself behind the wheel and pressed the starter. Revving the powerful engine he backed out onto the road and tore after the car ahead.

It wasn't long before the lights of the vehicle came into view. Ravenwood drew a deep breath and eased up on the gas. He slowed far enough back to not look suspicious. The car headed straight back into the heart of the city. As they made their way into busier areas, Ravenwood got a look at the car as it traveled down well lit streets. It was a newer Ford coupe, a nice car but not particularly expensive. He continued following it until it pulled up in front of an apartment building not far from the business district. He killed the roadster's light and pulled to the curb. A single man stepped out of the coupe and headed into the building. As he entered, Ravenwood got a good look at him in the light. He was a slightly built man with a receding hairline. It looked to Ravenwood from that distance that he had a thin beard. The strangest thing was that he seemed to blur in Ravenwood's sight for just a second. He reached the door and peered through the glass in time to see the elevator doors close on the man. He got a clear look at his face then and he would remember it. Was this Hartley? The outer door was locked. Over the door a sign proclaimed these the Yorkshire Apts. He looked around carefully and then exerting his mind and will opened the lock and entered the lobby.

He loitered a moment and watched the elevator dial above the doors. It stopped on six. He found the stairway and made his way quickly up to the sixth floor. There appeared to be a total of ten apartment doors on the floor. Ravenwood went from door to door stopping at each one to touch the door knob. He wondered what would happen if any occupants were to step out into the hallway and see him holding hands with a door knob, especially since he was wearing a dirty and ripped tuxedo, but fortunately the hallway remained empty. He was rewarded at the door of 6E. When he touched the door knob, it immediately grew very warm and his hand tingled. When he pushed out his senses he felt a troubling presence. Deciding it would be better to return after he had learned more, Ravenwood headed home.

Fortunately there were enough trees and brush between him and the road that he could not be seen.

The next morning, Ravenwood was ready to leave and find out more about the mysterious man he had followed from Hartley's house when the telephone rang. Sterling announced Inspector Stagg and handed him the receiver. He took it with a foreboding. "Good morning inspector. What can I do for you?"

"What's good about it? I need you down town right away, Ravenwood."

"Of course Inspector. Should I meet you at the station?

"No. City morgue, right away."

The click as he hung up was loud in Ravenwood's ear. As he put on his gloves and turned toward the door, he was blocked by Stirling holding up his battered and dirty tuxedo. "And what do you wish me to do with this, sir?"

Ravenwood reached out and touched the suit with the tip of his walking stick. "Burn it, and call my tailor to make an appointment for a fitting for a new tux." Stirling nodded as Ravenwood exited through the door. As he swung it closed, Ravenwood added, "And don't you dare tell him what happened to the last one."

This wasn't the first time Ravenwood had visited the city morgue, so it wasn't hard to find parking, sign in and be directed to the correct room. He found Inspector Stagg leaning against the morgue attendant's desk, munching his inevitable peanuts with the attendant shooting him dirty looks for the peanut debris being dropped on this otherwise spotless floor. Tugging off his gloves and placing them in his hat, he smiled at Stagg. "Well, Inspector, I don't expect you called me down here to give me any good news."

Stagg stood up and dusted his hands together. "'Fraid not, Blackstone, we've got another one." He gestured to the attendant, who got up and led them through a set of swinging doors into an inner room. It was very cool here and two walls were lined with small 3' x 3' refrigerator-like doors. He consulted a clipboard and then opened a lower door and slid out the sheet-covered figure on a long tray. Standing back he waved the two investigators in.

Stagg strode forward and uncovered the figure to its waist. The victim was a male, probably in his early thirties. He had dark hair and an olive complexion. Other than the large open incision in his chest, the most unusual thing about him was he was missing his left thumb. Ravenwood's chameleon-like eyes darkened as he leaned forward and felt a familiar taint of evil around the body. He scanned the chest wound carefully and looked up expectantly at Stagg.

Stagg recited, "This is Freddy 'The Thumb' Cantoni. He's lived here in town for some time. He did time up in Illinois for assault and was arrested several other times with no charges. The word is he's working for Anthony Lorenzo. Lorenzo's a former bootlegger with mob ties. He maintains a low profile here. We've had him under occasional surveillance but he doesn't seem to be up to any mob activities. I talked to him this morning and he claims he doesn't know Freddy here. By the way, we found his naked body in a downtown alley first thing this morning."

Ravenwood knew he had to proceed carefully here to avoid further suspicions. "Is there any kind of connection between this man and the first two victims?"

"No, and that kind of blows your theory out of the water. I told you this is the work of some kind of maniac with a 'Jack the Ripper complex.'"

Ravenwood nodded as if considering this. "Have you found any connections between the first two victims?"

Stagg scuffed his toe on the floor. "Well, yeah. It seems that Larsen and DeGraaf were involved in a lot of real estate deals, DeGraaf supplying the financing." He hesitated.

Ravenwood prompted him. "Anything else?"

Stagg rubbed his chin. "Yeah, we talked to Larsen's secretary. She confirmed that a few of Larsen's clients were upset over losing money. The most recent one was, uh," he consulted a notebook taken from his pocket, "Let's see, a Professor Hartley who teaches at the university. He's the one who has been calling the last couple of weeks. I guess he's been threatening a lawsuit lately."

Ravenwood tried hard not to nod or smile. At last the inspector was finally catching on. A few gentle nudges in the right direction and Ravenwood could stand back and let the law sort things out. He mildly inquired, "Has anyone thought about talking to Hartley? He might know more about Larsen and DeGraaf. He might even know how this man and Lorenzo fit into things."

Inspector Stagg shook his head, "Naw, that's a dead end. We checked on Hartley. He was killed a week ago."

Ravenwood was stunned. He made a tremendous effort and kept his face calm. His mind was racing. If Hartley was dead, who was living at his house? And who was killing and collecting hearts? Only Hartley would need them for his rituals.

Keeping his voice casual he asked, "Really, how did he die?"

Stagg shrugged, "The blotter shows that he was killed in a traffic accident on River Road last week during that big thunderstorm we had. Lightning hit a power pole. It fell on a truck, causing it to smash into two cars. One went into the river; Hartley was driving the other one. He was D.O.A. with head injuries. Matter of fact, he's down here now waiting for his next of kin to pick him up. I guess his sister's coming into town tomorrow to make arrangements."

Surprised, Ravenwood asked, "Really, can we take a look at the body?"

Stagg shrugged and looked at the morgue attendant. He also shrugged, consulted his clipboard and led the way across the room to another drawer which he opened and pulled out. He pulled back the sheet. Stagg and Ravenwood moved forward to take a look. They saw a tall, thin, middle-aged man with dark hair going gray and a neatly trimmed van dyke beard. The trauma to his head was obvious.

When he looked at the body, Ravenwood's vision blurred momentarily. Somehow, Hartley's body had an aura about it, and to Ravenwood the body carried a strong scent of evil. He stepped back and gathered his thoughts. "Well, if Hartley isn't responsible for the murders, it could still be he's the cause of all this. Perhaps Larsen and DeGraaf were running land schemes using Lorenzo's money as backing, and with unhappy investors like Hartley making waves, Lorenzo decided to tie up some loose ends." Ravenwood kept a straight face as he spun this little story for inspector Stagg.

Stagg grimaced. "Look, Ravenwood, Lorenzo is no saint, but we can't tie him to these weird murders. The only slight connection is his boy Freddy over there. These murders were committed by some maniac. We're checking hospitals now for escaped patients. I just called you down here to show you the newest body to blow up your cockeyed theory. Now get out of my hair. I got an insane killer to find." Ravenwood bowed and left without another word. Stagg would not be swayed without evidence biting him in the leg.

Ravenwood returned home and spent the rest of the day thinking. His main suspect Hartley was dead. Lorenzo was now the best suspect, but why would he murder and steal the heart of one of his own men? Professsor Hartley was the only one who would have a use for the hearts, but Hartley was dead. He had seen the body himself. And who was living in Hartley's house? Was it someone attempting to continue the professor's dark rituals? He decided he should speak with Hartley's sister when she arrived tomorrow. Perhaps she could shed light on who had access to Hartley's house. He also needed to follow up on the mysterious man he had followed the night before. After his date with Sophia he would do some investigating on that front.

After changing into evening wear, he drove the roadster to Sophia's home to pick her up. He had made reservations at one of most exclusive restaurants in town. While driving toward the center of town, Ravenwood gradually sensed he was being followed. He briefly considered doubling back in attempt to identify his pursuers, but decided that following him to a restaurant was innocent. What could they learn? At the restaurant, he surrendered the roadster to the parking valet and they checked their coats. They were then greeted by the maitre'de who expressed his pleasure at seeing Ravenwood once more and showed them to their table. Sophia was a good companion and Ravenwood thoroughly enjoyed dinner. They had finished desert and ordered coffee when he excused himself to use the lavatory. The restrooms were down a short hallway at the back of the building. He entered and was straightening his tux in front of the mirror as another man entered. Ravenwood immediately felt the chill on his neck that meant danger. He turned toward the newcomer and heard one of the stalls opening. Accompanied by a metal double click, a voice spoke quietly. "Don't move, you're covered."

He looked carefully over his shoulder and saw another man holding a short-barreled revolver pointed at him. Both men were wearing cheap suits and had the rough look that marked them as hired muscle. He started to raise his hands, but the first man, who also had produced a gun, said, "Keep your hands down. We're going to walk out of here, turn right and go to the back door. Don't talk to anyone, just smile and look normal. Got it?"

Not seeing any alternative, Ravenwood nodded. The first man opened the restroom door and glanced out. He nodded to his partner and exited. The second man jerked his head in the direction of the door, and Ravenwood followed with the second man just behind him. They passed a room where off-duty waiters took their breaks and a doorway to the kitchen before reaching the alley door. No one questioned them. Ravenwood followed the first man into the alley where yet another man waited with gun drawn.

Once the door closed behind them, they pushed Ravenwood against a wall and lined up in front of him. One spoke. "Alright, pal, we were sent to find out just who you are and what you're up to, so start talking."

"My name is Ravenwood," he calmly replied.

"Yeah, yeah. We know who you are and where you live. Now we want to know why you're snooping around Tony Lorenzo's place. You're not a cop. Are you some kind of private shamus? Who're you working for?

Ravenwood realized these were some of Lorenzo's hoods. They must have caught a glimpse of his license plate yesterday and Lorenzo must be suspicious, probably paranoid as well. "I'm just a private citizen. I sometimes work as a consultant to the local police." This caused some surprised looks among the three. One of the hoods spoke out of the corner of his mouth to the others. "He's lying. He's got to be the one who killed Freddy 'The Thumb.'"

Ravenwood reached his arms forward as if pleading and pitched his voice slightly higher. "I had nothing to do with that. Oh, thank God Inspector! You're just in time!" Influenced by "the voice," all three gunmen turned to look down the alley. Launching himself off the wall, Ravenwood jerked his Luger from its holster. He brought it crashing down on the head of one of the hoods. He then back handed the gun across the cheek of a second. The third man was swinging his gun around when Ravenwood crashed into him. He got hold of the hood's gun hand in his left hand while he shoved his automatic as hard as he could into the man's stomach. His breath came out in a whoosh. Gasping and unable to draw breath, he dropped his gun and slid to his knees holding his stomach.

Ravenwood saw that their disturbance had brought no attention to the alley. Gathering up his opponents' guns, he tossed them into a garbage bin and holstering his automatic, he pulled open the door to the restaurant. One of the men was still gasping for breath, one was stirring slightly and the third was still unconscious. He walked briskly down the hall and across the floor of the restaurant. Approaching the maitre d' he said, "I have been called away on an emergency. Can you put dinner on my account and I will come by tomorrow and settle up?" The maître de bowed slightly and replied, "Of course, Mr. Ravenwood. Your credit is always good here. Take your time." Ravenwood then pressed a bill into his hand and smiled. "Please have my car brought around at once."

Moving quickly back to their table, he gathered up Sophia. "My dear, I'm afraid I've been called away on official business. I'll drop you at home." The surprised girl acquiesced and let Ravenwood shepherd her to the front door, stopping only to collect their coats from the coat check. Once on the sidewalk, Ravenwood tried to look casual as he waited impatiently for his car. He knew it would not be long until the gunmen in the alley pulled themselves together and came in angry pursuit. He smiled at Sophia's casual chatter until the welcome sight of his roadster pulling up distracted her. Bundling her into the car he drove casually away from the restaurant and was just relaxing when words formed in his mind:

"Danger is approaching." Glancing instinctively in the mirror, he could see a pair of headlights that looked to be coming fast. He pressed down on the gas and the powerful roadster leaped forward. He passed a slower car and again looked to see to the pursuing car still coming. At his side, Sophia looked at him. "What's wrong darling? Why are we in such a hurry?"

"I'm afraid we have some unpleasant men following us Sophia. I need to concentrate and I would appreciate it if you didn't distract me." He turned the wheel sharply and screeched into a turn on two wheels. Sophia paled and grabbed onto a strap to maintain her balance. Swerving around traffic, Ravenwood tried to open the distance between them and their pursuers, but busy streets and slower traffic kept him from utilizing the supercharged roadster's full power. The pursuing car doggedly held on as they twisted and turned down city streets. Finally deciding to break the stalemate, Ravenwood made for the edge of town where he could open the distance.

Traffic lightened as they reached the outskirts of the city. Unfortunately, flashes of light in his mirror and the whine of bullets past the roadster told Ravenwood that their foes had also changed their tactics. As the wing mirror to Ravenwood's left shattered, he heard "That which cannot be borne must be changed." A plan quickly formed, and he slowed the powerful car. The pursuing car rapidly closed the distance. Glancing to the side, he could see Sophia's face was white with fear. He smiled in reassuringly in return.

As they caught up, his pursuers swerved their car out to come alongside the roadster, obviously with the intention of shooting them or forcing them of the road. Ravenwood waited patiently. As the pursuing car drew alongside, he could see the driver hunched over the wheel and a man next to him holding a gun. At this point, Ravenwood thrust his hand outward toward the car's driver and called out in his mind, "Learned one, I need your help!" He felt a jolt of power in his arm. Simultaneously his opponent's car served out of control as the steering wheel spun out of the driver's hands. The car swerved onto the shoulder spewing gravel. It tore through a fence and crashed directly into a medium-sized tree. Momentarily slowing the roadster, Ravenwood looked over his shoulder. The other car was only partially illuminated by its one remaining unshattered headlight. No one moved in the car. He accelerated and drove away.

The shaken Sophia was silent for the rest of the trip to her family's home. As he pulled up in the curving driveway, she finally spoke. "Those men, why were they trying to hurt us?"

Ravenwood answered carefully, "I'm not sure. I think it might have something to do with a crime I am assisting the police with. I am sorry you had to go through that. It was not the evening I planned."

Sophia did not answer. Ravenwood walked her to the door and bid her good night. As he drove away, he wondered if he would hear from her again. If he didn't, it wouldn't the first time.

※※※

He headed back toward the center of town and drove directly to the Yorkshire apartments. Pressing the bell marked manager, he waited. Soon the casually dressed manager arrived at the door putting on his jacket. Unlocking the door, he asked Ravenwood about his business. Knowing he made a good impression in his formal , Ravenwood spun the man a story how he had been helped by a stranger. He described the man he had followed and explained that he wanted to thank the unnamed stranger who had helped him. Impressed, the manager told him that he must be describing Mr. Coogan, the accountant, who lived 6E. When Ravenwood asked to go up to his apartment the manager told him that he thought Coogan was out. In fact, he had not been around much at all in the last week. Ravenwood smiled and said he would just slip his card under the door with a thank you written on it. The manager smiled and admitted him.

Quickly making his way to the sixth floor, Ravenwood had no trouble unlocking the door of 6E. Inside, he caught a faint sense of evil but nothing overwhelming. The apartment was modestly furnished, just what he would expect from an accountant. He scouted through it, quickly finishing in the kitchen where the refrigerator had a shimmery aura about it. Opening it, he found little inside. There was no fresh food at all, just a few eggs and several bottles of mustard, ketchup, etc., confirming the manager's statement that Coogan had not been around his apartment much lately. Noticing a spot on the floor of the refrigerator, Ravenwood squatted down. On closer examination, he could see the spot was a small puddle of dried blood. There were also signs of blood on the lowest metal shelf. Reaching out to touch the dried blood, Ravenwood somehow knew instantly that it was human blood. He closed the refrigerator and after one last look around left the apartment.

He felt a new suspect had been added. Obviously this man Coogan had something to do with Hartley, and appeared to be spending time at

Hartley's house. Could he have been involved in Hartley's dark rituals? Tomorrow he would meet and question Hartley's sister about Hartley and Coogan. If he could find a connection, Inspector Stagg would be there to carry the ball. He was not followed on the way home.

In the morning, Ravenwood called Inspector Stagg to find out where and when he was meeting Hartley's sister. Stagg was suspicious, but told him to be at the train station to meet the 1 p.m. train. Dressed conservatively, Ravenwood was there early. Just before one he saw Stagg enter the station and started forward to greet him when his attention was drawn to another figure striding across the platform. Quickly he faded out of sight behind a pillar. He watched fascinated as the unmistakable figure of the balding Coogan came to a stop just feet away from the stocky figure of Inspector Stagg. Stagg, not knowing who he was, paid him no mind at all. Ravenwood watched Coogan closely, just as yesterday, the man seemed to be somewhat blurry whenever Ravenwood looked directly at him. He had never seen such a phenomenon and was not sure what it meant. Coogan was dressed in a blue suit and appeared to be growing a small beard. Within minutes the expected train chugged slowly into the station. There was the usual confusion as dozens of people disembarked and dozens more stepped forward to greet them. Stagg seemed to know just who to look for because he stepped forward quickly as a thin gray haired lady was helped down the step by a porter. Surprisingly, he tipped his hat and introduced himself in a loud voice easily heard over the platform noise. Coogan had also stepped toward the gray hired woman but skidded to a halt as the inspector stepped forward and introduced himself. Instead, he quickly turned off and headed down the platform. He stepped behind a loaded baggage cart and watched Stagg and the Hartley woman.

Stagg spent several minutes talking to the woman. Ravenwood was far enough away that he could catch only bits of their conversation, but he did hear the both Larsen's and DeGraaf's name mentioned. The woman's voice grew louder at these names; it was apparent they upset her. During this time, a porter appeared to wheel away the cart. Coogan slipped behind a nearby pillar and continued watching. Eventually,Stagg tipped his hat and turned to leave. He checked his watch and looked disgustedly around. Ravenwood had to duck back quickly to not be seen; when he looked again the inspector was gone.

Coogan wasted no time. He was quickly at Hartley's sister's side, introducing himself and taking her bag from the porter's hands. Ravenwood strolled after them as Coogan quickly ushered her to the door. He was just behind them as they walked down the steps to the sidewalk. He turned and pretended to hail a cab as the two entered the same car that Coogan had been driving two nights before. As the car passed, he noted the license number and then sprinted across the street to his own car. As Ravenwood pulled a quick U-turn he noted a black sedan pulling out a few cars back. He lost Coogan's car in the traffic around downtown but wasn't worried. He knew where they had to be going. He headed directly toward Hartley's isolated house. He noted that the black car from the station was still behind him although it was staying a respectful distance behind. Once near Hartley's house, he pulled into the overgrown driveway he had used before. Avoiding the heavy brush, he walked along the road and found a spot behind a large tree where he could watch the house. Coogan's car was there and he could see movement in the house. He continued to watch. The only interruption was when a black sedan with two men inside crept slowly down the road. It paused near his parked roadster and moved on. It came to a complete halt opposite Hartley's house for a minute or more, and then moved on. Ravenwood continued to watch for almost an hour. He saw occasional movement at the windows but nothing more. Making a decision he walked briskly back to his car and headed home. The black car followed him back to town, but somewhere it peeled off on its own.

While eating a hearty snack, Ravenwood noted the sky darkening. It would be a cloudy night, good for observing the house. Before changing, he went to the room of his mentor. He entered the dimly lit room and seated himself cross-legged from the wise man. The silence was heavy until the Nameless One spoke suddenly. "A storm approaches this night. Evil comes with it. A man will attempt to breach the walls of this reality. No one but you, my son, can stop this from happening." He waited but the old one said no more, and Ravenwood quietly left the room.

By dark, Ravenwood had changed into his dark clothing. He checked his automatic and thrust it into its holster beneath his wind breaker and was ready. Once in his roadster, he left the Sussex Arms and drove slowly through town. When he was sure that the black car was again following him, he located a convenient drug store and went in. He dialed police headquarters and asked for Inspector Stagg. When Stagg came on the line Ravenwood didn't let him launch into his usual tirade, "Don't talk, just listen." He then told Stagg that he had figured things out. He told him that Larsen and DeGraaf had been running land schemes with Lorenzo's money. Hartley lost a lot of money in one of these schemes, perhaps others as well. That tied them all together. There was also a man named Coogan involved, but Ravenwood was not sure how. Perhaps he was another victim in the land schemes. Perhaps he was behind the murders and mutilations. He then gave Coogan's license plate number and address and told him to carefully search the apartment for clues. He also told the spluttering inspector that something was probably going on at Hartley's house. He then quickly hung up.

Once again in his car, he drove carefully across town and out the road to Hartley's house. He parked his car closer to the house this time and waited inside for a time. He then got out and snuck through the trees to where he could observe the house. It was dimly lit and there was no movement at any of the windows. He again took his time before creeping across the lawn to crouch beside the house. The night was dark and thunder rumbled in the distance. Making sure he was on the side visible from the road, Ravenwood tried several windows. They were all locked, and he took his time selecting one before using his mental powers to slide back the catch. Pushing it open, he boosted himself up and into it. He then closed it and crouched by it, staring toward the road. He didn't see anything, but was sure that the men following had seen every move. Standing up, he moved carefully through the house. There were a few dim lights on, but otherwise the entire above-ground floors were empty. He moved to the kitchen and listened at the basement door. He could hear multiple muffled voices. He also could feel the evil flowing under and around the cracks of the door. It was as the Nameless One had said. The evil was happening here.

Ravenwood quietly pulled the door open a crack. The voices came through more clearly. He then turned and made his way across the house to the side opposite the road and opened a window. He dropped silently to the ground, closed the window and moved off. It took a little doing with the darkness and clouds, but he finally decided what direction to take and set off through the trees toward the ruined building he had found. It was dark and the underbrush grew thicker until it was ripping at his clothes. He sighed as he forced his way along. He was being very hard on his wardrobe this week.

It was so dark that he collided with a waist-high wall before he realized

"Don't talk, just listen."

he had reached his goal. He rubbed his stinging knee for a moment before he eased himself over the wall and into the ruined building. Now that he was somewhat concealed, he got down on his knees and turned on his flashlight. Keeping it shielded, he searched the ground. The ground was covered in leaves and other rotting matter he had to scrape aside. Occasionally, he came across a rusting piece of metal. When the ground felt solid he gave it a hard rap. Eventually he found a hard placed that gave off a muffled metallic sound. He grabbed the remains of an old board. It was rotting but held together well enough as he used to it to scrape soil from atop the metal door. Eventually he had it clear enough to attempt to open it. He braced his legs and tugged upward. He was rewarded with a loud screech. Gritting his teeth against the sound, he heaved again. The door gave and swung upward a foot. Shifting his grip to the door's edge, he pulled it wide open.

Using the flashlight, he went down the steps into the tunnel. Thunder rumbled close as he disappeared into the earth. He drew his Luger and started carefully along the passage. After seventy steps, he stopped and turned off the light. He could hear muffled sounds and could make out dim light around the edges of the small door leading into the basement vault. He edged closer until he could put his ear to the door. He definitely could hear a rhythmic voice. The feeling of evil was nearly overpowering. He pushed the door gently. It opened a few inches, but he stopped when it gave off a small squeak. He could hear the voice more clearly. It was a male voice chanting in some strange language that Ravenwood did not understand, although the words themselves chilled him. Risking more squeaks he pushed door open far enough where he could lean his head into the room and see more of the vault.

The vault was illuminated by several large candles set in niches in the walls, a free-standing multi-candled candelabra and three-legged braziers provided adequate but shadowy illumination. The table in the center of the painted circle now held the obviously dead figure of a woman. Dark stains that must be blood were all over the body. He couldn't tell from here, but Ravenwood felt sure it was Hartley's sister. His knuckles closed fiercely on his gun butt. He turned his attention to the other figures in the room. Coogan, wearing a dark, floor-length robe, was standing near the table, chanting in a loud voice. He held something dark in his hand.

He tossed it into a blazing brazier and reached for something else that could only be a human heart. He lifted it overhead and began to chant again. Except for another figure in identical robe who looked familiar, the basement seemed empty.

Ravenwood had seen enough. He pushed the door wide with a further loud screech and pushed into the room, covering it with his pistol. "Stand where you are," he commanded. Ravenwood's pistol swung gently between the men, menacing them both.

"Alright, Coogan, if that is your name, this hellish ceremony is over. Whatever you're attempting to do will never happen."

Coogan turned, his hand holding the heart still raised. He seemed surprised but unafraid. Slowly he lowered his arm. "Who are you?"

Ravenwood held the pistol steady. "It doesn't matter. What matters is I have come to put a stop to whatever devilish sacrifice you are performing. So put that heart down, Coogan, and you lead the way up stairs, your friend too."

Coogan looked at him curiously and smiled. "You have no idea what is going on here, do you? I was the man known as Coogan but he is no longer. Now I am again Professor Hartley. If death could not stop me, do you think you can?"

Ravenwood felt a chill down his back. "Hartley is dead. I saw his body."

"You saw the body I once inhabited. There was an auto accident; I was badly injured and Coogan drowned in the river but was revived. I died too, just as Coogan was revived. Somehow my essence moved to Coogan's body and I live."

Ravenwood was stunned at this revelation. He felt he knew the answer but he had to ask, "And what happened to Coogan's spirit?"

"It ceased to exist. Now I am Hartley."

That explained a lot of things. "So you decided to take your revenge on the men who cheated you and use their hearts in your rituals? Why did you kill one of Lorenzo's men instead of him?"

Coogan/Hartley frowned, "He was too well guarded. I went there to take his heart, but I was discovered. I killed one of his men and took his heart instead."

Ravenwood pointed to the woman's corpse on the table, "And this poor woman, your own sister?"

Staring down at the heart in his hand, the sorcerer frowned, "When I told her what had happened, she threatened to go to the police. I couldn't let her do that, and I needed a fourth heart to complete the ritual."

"Well, you killed her for nothing. We're going to call the police now."

Holding the heart up in the air once more, he laughed, "The police won't believe you. They think Hartley is dead. But it is all moot. When I complete the ceremony, I will have all the power I need. I will be untouchable." Turning, he shouted out a foreign word and threw the remaining heart into the blazing brazier. Immediately, dark smoke welled out of the brazier. It grew into a small cloud centered above the now dim flame. Ravenwood raised his pistol to shoot, but his attention was drawn to the stairway. He could see light on the stairs and heard multiple feet clattering down the stairs. "Great, now they come," he thought as he backed against a wall.

The dark cloud of smoke had grown until it dominated the center of the room; a darker center had formed within it. On the stairs there were shouts of surprise. Four men, all carrying guns, had appeared on the stairs. Ravenwood recognized the bandaged head of one of Lorenzo's goons. The man in front shouted, "What the devil's going on here."

His attention drawn back to the center of the room, Ravenwood understood his shock. The cloud had grown to fill the center of the room. He could not see Hartley or his friend, but he could hear voices on the other side of the cloud. The dark center of the cloud had hardened into a frightening ugly shape that seemed to move by itself, and a feeling of terror was fast filling the room. Time to go. Ravenwood aimed carefully and fired twice, knocking over one of the flaming braziers. The floor was smooth concrete, and flaming debris scattered. He then scattered a couple of quick shots toward the stairs and ducked. Multiple shots responded from Lorenzo's goons. Bullets ricocheted around the room. The candelabra was knocked to the floor. There were curses and shouts. Bending low, Ravenwood ran bent over toward the stairs. He brushed against someone in the dark and smoke but shouldered past and kept moving forward. By the time he reached the stairs, there was pandemonium. The hellish shape at the center of the cloud, and hardened into a huge figure; it was now roaring like a dozen lions combined. In addition, people were screaming and bullets fired wildly ricocheted off walls. As he scuttled up the stairs he could see the huge figure smash a man into a wall with one clawed hand. He reached the kitchen, slammed the door shut and turned the key in the lock. Knowing the flimsy wooden door wouldn't do much to stop the hell-spawned creature in the basement, he looked around for something to block the door. Chairs wouldn't do. The stove: too heavy to move.

Then inspiration struck. Holstering his Luger, he jammed a chair under the door knob and ran to the gas range. One strong heave moved a corner of it out from the wall enough to reach behind. Thrusting his arm between the wall and the stove, he grasped the flexible metal gas line. He gave it a strong jerk, but nothing gave, a stronger heave and he felt something move. He braced his leg against the stove and prepared for a mighty heave. A terrible bubbling scream from the basement gave him strength as he wrenched backwards with all he had. The gas line gave way with a snap so sudden that Ravenwood went sprawling on the floor. Jumping up, he could already smell the acrid stench of the escaping gas filling the room. He rushed into the dining room flipping on light switches as he passed. In the hall, he continued flipping every light switch he saw. Turning, he tore back through the house, holding his breath as he ran through the kitchen. He exited the house through the back door, taking time to close it softly. A touch and a few seconds of mental concentration, and he heard the lock click. Leaping off the back porch he raced for the trees.

Deliberately slowing his breath, he drew his Luger and braced it across his arm while leaning against the large tree. He could still hear distant screams and crashes from the house. He waited. Timing would be crucial. The longer he waited the more gas filled the house but he couldn't wait too long. He could not risk that hellish demon escaping into an unsuspecting world; the consequences were too terrible to contemplate.

A loud crashing came from the house and he could see debris flying about the kitchen. Ravenwood took aim on the overhead light fixture in the kitchen. It would be difficult shot from twenty-five or more yards but he dared not miss. A huge dark shape could be seen moving in the kitchen. His finger tightened. . .and without warning fire belched out of every window and door of the house. Hot wind buffeted Ravenwood as the shockwave and crushing noise rolled over him. Instantly the house was heavily on fire. He stepped out from behind the tree. Small pieces of smoldering debris were landing around him. His pistol hung at the end of his arm as he watched in awe the flames consume the old mansion. Black smoke rolled into the dark sky. Ravenwood holstered his pistol under his wind breaker and turned away.

Making his way quickly to his roadster he paused before slipping behind the wheel. Looking back, he could see flames climbing over the trees. It was obvious that fire equipment would not be in time to save the house. He just hoped that fire wouldn't spread through the trees to other dwellings. He had turned onto the main road and was several miles from the burning house when the first fire truck passed him going the other way.

Driving back to the city he began to reflect on Coogan/Hartley's final victim, his own sister. Could he have taken action sooner and saved her? As those melancholy thoughts began to take root, he heard the Nameless One again. "We can only ever do our best, my son. As gifted as you have become, in the end you remain only one man. Her spirit is at rest as you have avenged her. Be content in that fact."

Ravenwood accepted the words, shrugged off his ennui and concentrated on the road ahead.

Ravenwood was reading the newspaper at his desk the next afternoon while he sipped brandy. He heard the doorbell ring. It did not take a mystic to realize it must be the intrepid inspector Stagg. Sterling entered the room but before he could announce the visitor, Stagg brushed past him. The inspector looked like he had had a very bad night. His rumpled suit was covered in black ash and one sleeve was torn. His hands were dirty and here was a smudge of soot on one cheek.

"Alright, Ravenwood, I want. . . "

Ravenwood cut in smoothly, "Would you like a brandy, Inspector? You look like you could use it."

Stunned, Stagg stuttered, "Uh, what? No, I don't want a brandy! I want to know what you had to do with last night."

What do you mean, Inspector?"

"I mean the fire and explosion at Professor Hartley's house. That's what I mean. I've been out there ever since the call came in last night. It's a mess. They're still digging bodies out of the ashes. Now, I know you've gotta be in on it. I got your message and you know what's going on here." He repeatedly stabbed his finger at Ravenwood as if it were a spear.

Ravenwood leaned forward and feigned surprise and interest, "Fire, explosion, at Hartley's house? What happened?"

That's what I want to know. You seem to know so much about what's going on around here."

Ravenwood sipped at his brandy and asked, "Do you know what caused the explosion?"

Stagg looked suddenly tired and shrugged. "The fire marshal says it was probably a gas explosion. It happened about eight o'clock last night. Neighbors heard the explosion going off. It's pretty isolated, and by the time the first fire engines got there it was too late. The place is nothing but ashes and it looks like nobody got out. What's left of the house collapsed into the basement. They'll be pulling bodies out for days."

Nodding his sympathy Ravenwood asked, "Do you know who the victims are yet?"

Stagg sagged exhaustedly into a chair. "Not for sure, some of them will probably never be identified, but we can guess. We found two cars registered to Tony Lorenzo, so we think he and a few of his boys were in the house. Also, Hartley's sister and butler are missing. We also found a rental car hired by that guy Coogan you told us about. We checked his apartment and found human blood stains in his refrigerator. Oh, we also found the connection between him and Hartley. They were in an . . ."

". . . accident together last week," Ravenwood finished.

Stagg glared at him. "How did you know that? And don't give me any of your hocus pocus."

Ravenwood shrugged, "I followed him from Larsen's office to Hartley's house the other day. I then did some checking and found the connection. Do you think Coogan was behind the murders?"

Stagg stood up. "Yeah, he was involved somehow ,but I don't know how. If he didn't die in the fire, we'll find him." He looked hard at Ravenwood. "You know more about this than you're letting on. One of these days your parlor tricks are going to get you in trouble." He turned to go. As he reached the door, Ravenwood mildly asked, "Are you sure you don't want a drink, Inspector?" Inspector Stagg stiffened and threw one last glare over his shoulder before storming from the penthouse. Ravenwood could hear the slam of the front door from the study. He picked up his brandy and strolled onto the balcony where he sipped the smooth liquid slowly.

The End

THE WRITING OF "HEART OF DARKNESS"

Writing "Heart of Darkness" was kind of like a sudden squall on the ocean. On a clear day it came out of nowhere: there was surprise, a bit of confusion, and for a little while a whole lot was happening. And just as soon as it showed up it was over and the sky was shining again, leaving one with that slightly unreal feeling of, "Whoa. What just happened?"

It started this way; I have been working on a series of stories about a swashbuckling adventurer set in pre-revolutionary America. I've written several short stories and novelettes, and decided I would start looking around for publishers to submit some things to. While researching on the internet, I stumbled across Ron Fortier's website. Recognizing his name as an adventure author, I wrote asking him for the addresses of some publishers. At that time, I thought it was a personal website and did not realize he was a publisher and editor himself.

Ron explained what he was doing and graciously offered to look at one of my stories. I was elated and sent him off a short story. Through a series of Abbott and Costello-like missteps we lost contact, and when we did resume correspondence, he didn't remember me or my story (by the way, this is all in a days' work for a freelance writer). We managed to quickly sort things out, and Ron not only found my story, he read and liked it.

Although my story wasn't something Ron was able to use immediately, he did like my writing enough to inquire if I would be interested in writing a story for Airship 27 about one of their current characters. He didn't have to ask twice. A flurry of emails back and forth ensued. We agreed on a character and I came away with an assignment. The amazing thing was all this happened in a matter of hours. So I started the day with a professional editor not even remembering me or my submission (another occupational hazard of writing), and ended it with a wonderful assignment to write a story about a classic pulp character from the 1930s.

I was so excited that I dove right in on this project. I had a detailed 2400 word synopsis within twenty-four hours and immediately started on "Heart of Darkness" (the original working title was "Heart Ache"). The writing went quickly, more quickly than even I expected. I wrote "Heart of Darkness" in six days, averaging more than 2500 words a day. One day I actually broke my personal best with just over 3,000 words. Of course, writing quickly is in the finest tradition of pulp literature. With tight deadlines and writing multiple characters for multiple magazines, many of the legendary pulp writers wrote prodigious amounts in amazingly short periods. I remember reading an interview with Walter Gibson (author of more than 200 Shadow novels) where he talked about writing many of his Shadow novels at a rate of five- to ten-thousand words a day. At any rate, the story wrote quickly and very naturally with no problems of any kind. It was a little long but a quick tightening of my prose and smoothing out of a few cumbersome passages and it was ready to go off to Ron.

Why did "Heart of Darkness" go so quickly? Well, much of the stuff I have been writing, while set in another century, is very similar in theme. Basically, I have been writing a lot of adventure/mystery with a healthy dose of supernatural horror thrown in. Substitute guns and cars for swords and horses and it was then easy to take one of my plot ideas and transplant it to the 1930s. I have a whole lot of ideas for adventure horror stories; cults, shape shifters, witchcraft and necromancy to name a few. I get ideas from all over; television, movies books, news. I mix and match ideas to come up with original and I hope interesting story plots and it seems to work (fingers crossed).

So, that's how "Heart of Darkness" came about. It was certainly a surprise. I had no idea when I wrote Ron that morning that within hours I would be off on a wonderful new adventure, but it turned out to be a heck of a ride and I'm pleased I got to write this story.

As a boy I read a lot of books and not a few pulps. It wasn't until much later as an adult that I found out that many of the well-known authors whom I had read with pleasure got their start writing for those beat up old magazines I found in second-hand stores and trunks. I don't claim to be in a class with any of those authors (in fact, I think of myself as a writer rather than an author), but it does give me a warm connected feeling to be able to say, "I've written a pulp story about a classic pulp character." If it was good enough for Walter Gibson, Raymond Chandler or even Robert Heinlein, then I guess I'm in very good company.

I had a lot of fun writing "Heart of Darkness" I hope you enjoy it as much I enjoyed writing it.

❋ ❋ ❋

GENE MOYERS - studied European and Medieval history at the University of Oregon. He is a former U.S. Army armor crewman. He worked in the high tech industry for some time and ran a store front and internet hobby shop for several years.

An avid military gamer and role player his favorite game was Daredevils role playing set in the 1930s. His love affair with the 1930s and pulps in particular stems from his first reading of a Shadow novel as a boy. Although interested in writing since a teen, he did not turn to serious writing until 2000. He is the co-author of GURPS Crusades published by Steve Jackson Games. When not working on Airship 27 projects, he is busy writing horror adventures for his swashbuckling character set in Colonial America.

Gene currently lives in Beaverton, Oregon, with his wife and three lazy dogs.

RAVENWOOD
SPECIAL EDITION

"Jazzy"

by Ron Fortier

JAZZY

By Ron Fortier

Ravenwood poured cream into his coffee and watched it transform the hot black liquid into swirling pool of a soft brown color. It reminded him immediately of his mother's eyes; one of the few lasting memories he had of her. She and his father had died when he was a small child in the Orient. Medical missionaries, they had been treating villagers in a plague-ridden locale when they both succumbed to the disease.

The memory was a cherished one. Tender brown eyes that had showered love on him for too short a time.

Ravenwood stirred the coffee with his spoon and then took a slow sip. The taste was both hardy and smooth; delicious as ever. He surveyed his surroundings. Of all the mysteries in the universe, this had the be the most puzzling; that the best coffee in all of New York City was to be had in a greasy-spoon diner called MURPHY'S on the west side of 7th Avenue several blocks south of Times Square.

It was after two in the morning and the place was deserted except for Jake, an old Negro short-order cook, and Wanda, a heavy-set brunette waitress who occupied her time doing crossword puzzles at the far end of the counter. Jake, for the most part, stayed busy baking pastries in the back kitchen; from bagels to donuts. These were all intended for the breakfast crowd who would daily invade the small, rectangular shaped eatery at the first light of dawn.

Ravenwood had discovered the diner years earlier upon his return home; a wealthy young man about to launch his career as an Occult Investigator. So much had happened since then, arriving back in America with his Tibetan mentor, the wise and mysterious monk he knew only as the Nameless One. Shortly thereafter he'd hired Sterling; the British gentlemen's gentlemen and gourmet chef to oversee his swank, Manhattan penthouse suite. In the past decade, he and his two associates had confronted all manner of bizarre occurrences; fought both human and demonic monsters while at the same time protecting the blissfully ignorant citizens of their wonderful city.

We're a strange family, we three. Ravenwood smiled at his own musings and started to take another drink of his rich coffee.

The door to the diner banged open and two customers entered; swept in by a cool gust of air. The first was a young girl with midnight black hair that was tied in a ponytail and half hidden beneath a man's woolen cap tucked down to hide her face. Ravenwood guessed her to be fifteen or sixteen whereas the person behind her was taller and older. This one, also female, wore a heavy black cloak and hood with black leather gloves and carried a worn, brown carpetbag that looked heavy. He assumed she was the girl's mother.

"Gosh, it's bloody cold out there," the teenager said as she beat her own gloved hands together.

She had a European accent with a strong Germanic flavor. Perhaps, Austria...or Transylvania. Ravenwood continued to enjoy his coffee while at the same time mentally sizing up these late night women.

"Springtime in the big city," Wanda explained as she stepped forward with two well-worn menus in her hand. "Would you girls like a booth or you can sit up at the counter." She waved her hand at the near empty interior. "Wherever is fine with me."

At that the woman reached up and pulled the hood off her head.

Ravenwood's breath caught in his throat as her beautiful face was revealed. She possessed an old world classical beauty of smooth alabaster skin with fine chiseled features, full red lips, a sharp Roman nose and dark, delicately shaped eyebrows over two large eyes. Her hair, like her daughter's, was jet black with a few streaks of gray peeking through. It was shoulder length and appeared uncombed.

He sensed an unsettling urgency about her.

In the process of lowering her hood, the woman had turned her head to survey their surroundings and for a fleeting second her eyes locked with his. Even from this distance their vibrant jade green color shined.

"A booth will do nicely, thank you." Her voice was cultured, confident and mature.

Wanda started to usher them towards the area where Ravenwood was seated when the woman stopped her. "Perhaps a booth to our right so as to not disturb the gentlemen's privacy."

Wanda shrugged her shoulders and turned on her heels. "No problem, dearie. Just you and your girl pick out whatever booth you'd like."

The woman nodded and followed her but not before glancing at Ravenwood one final time. He smiled demurely and nodded acknowledging her thoughtfulness for which he received a guarded smile in return. Although appreciating her gesture he suddenly felt as if he'd been robbed.

He would not have minded her presence at all, he realized. It had been a long time since any woman had elicited such a reaction from him.

Wanda led them to one of the six tables occupying the opposite section of the diner and stopped at mid-point. "How's this?"

"Fine, thank you..." Before the woman could finish, the teenager had moved past her and dropped onto the red vinyl seat to the left of the table, patting her hands on the clean Formica top.

"No, Jazemara, the other side."

For a second the pretty young girl frowned and quickly slid out off the cushioned seat and sat in its opposite twin.

"Thank you," the woman sat in the spot vacated by her daughter and set down the carpetbag beside her.

She didn't want her back to the entrance. The thought came to Ravenwood unbidden. But he knew instinctively he was right. Who were they and what were they doing out at this late hour? The anxiousness he'd sensed from the woman and her desire to face the diner's only main door. What was she afraid of? Were they running away from someone? Or something?

After glancing at the torn cardboard menu, the alluring woman looked up at Wanda and asked for her advice. "My daughter and I are very hungry. We'd like something hot and filling ...that will not take too long to prepare."

"Well, Jake still has some of tonight's meatloaf on the stove. He could cut you up some of that and put it on rye bread with mustard. Wouldn't take no time at all."

"Do you have any pie?" the girl asked, pulling off her cap and then her gloves.

"Sure thing, honey. We got apple and cherry. They're real yummy."

The daughter looked to her mother questioningly.

"Very well," she agreed, then gave Wanda their order for two meatloaf sandwiches to be followed by two slices of apple pie. "I'll have some coffee as well and you can bring my daughter some hot chocolate if you have any."

"I think I can rustle some up," the waitress said collecting the menus before she walked away and disappeared into the swinging door behind the counter. Her voice could be heard giving the cook their request.

Ravenwood took another drink of his coffee and mentally shrugged. He had to stop playing detective all the time. The way he had inspected the raven-haired woman and her child was silly. They were strangers of no concern to him and here he was letting his curiosity get the best of him; to include his unexpected feelings of arousal.

You are in danger, my son.

The thought that suddenly popped into his head was not his own. He recognized it immediately as a psychic warning from the Nameless One.

How? From where? He closed his eyes, attempting to receive his mentor's ethereal warning clearer.

The woman in black…beware!

There was a clinking sound followed by a rolling noise and then something small bumped into his left shoe. His eyes snapped opened, glanced down in time to see a round, silver medallion the size of a half-dollar fall over on the floor.

"I'm sorry, sir, it got away from me." The young girl had rushed over to retrieve what was obviously her coin.

He leaned over and picked it up and then held it up for her. "No need to apologize, young lady. Here is your runaway medallion." He noticed there was a German cross-embossed on its surface with words imprinted around the circumference. "Courage, loyalty and honor."

"You speak German?" The girl took the coin and smiled surprised by his ability to translate the inscription. Her eyes were infinite pools of deep blue-gray.

"Languages are a hobby of mine." He pointed to the coin. "That's a war medal, I believe. Awarded for exemplary courage in combat."

"It was my father's," she said. "Though I never met him. He died in the war. He was a famous flier. Mother says he was very brave."

"Then he has left you a proud legacy…."

"Mein Gott, your eyes!" the girl gasped realizing for the first time their strangeness. "They are not the same color!"

Ravenwood smiled. It was a reaction he was all too familiar with, having experienced it countless times in his life. "I have a medical condition known as hetrochromia, a difference of coloration in the irises. What are they now?"

The girl took a second to reply. "The left one is brown and the right one is a bright blue. What do you mean 'now.' Do they change?"

"Sometimes. Mine is a very rare case beyond the norm. My eyes change colors at random…without any warnings."

"Does it hurt?"

It was such a sweet and innocent question. Ravenwood was quickly becoming enamored with this girl. "No, not at all. In fact I'm never aware of when it happens…unless someone else points it out to me."

"Jazemara!" The girl's mother was noticeably annoyed. "Stop bothering the gentleman and return to your seat."

"Yes, mother." She started to comply with the order then suddenly leaned over and said in a conspiratorial whisper, "I'm Jazzy. Nice to meet you."

"I am Ravenwood and the pleasure is all mine, Jazzy."

Wanda was coming out of the swinging kitchen door just as the girl was returning to her seat to face her mother who merely looked at her with a stern expression. It spoke louder than any words of corrections.

"Here you go, ladies," Wanda said carefully placing the two plates down before the duo. "Two meatloaf sandwiches. Give me a second and I'll get your drinks."

As the friendly waitress started back around the corner, the front door opened and three men crowded into the diner. All of them were tall and brutish in appearance, wearing dark, soiled clothing and hats pulled down over their heads.

"Evening, gents," Wanda said stopping by the counter. "Just find a place to sit and I'll be right with you."

"That shall not be necessary," the closest man replied in a high-pitched voice. He looked at Jazzy and her mother. "We see what we've come for."

And with that, he reached out with his right hand and swiped it across Wanda's throat.

The second blood gushed from the woman's sliced throat, it splashed over her killer's face and he grinned, holding his hand to expose the inch long, razor sharp fingernails now coated in red. The mortally injured woman clutched at her severed throat trying to staunch the fountaining blood but it was useless.

She was dead long before she dropped to the floor.

Ravenwood came out of his booth clutching his silver tipped cane in his left hand.

One of the three intruders turned to him, tearing off his hat to expose his bald head and milk-white pallor. The fangs in his mouth accentuated his gaunt face. He was a vampire like his two companions.

"Really, a stick?" The monster charged him.

Ravenwood waited until the last possible moment and then reaching across his body, jerked the hidden rapier from its wooden scabbard and impaled the creature through the heart. The vampire was transfixed, his blood red eyes looking down at the steel in his chest. He snarled and grabbed for it with both hands.

"This will not stop me!"

He began to pull the blade from his body.

At the same time, across the diner, the other two vampires had turned their attention to the two women who were their real target.

"At long last, you are ours," the leader of the undead trio bragged as he approached their table slowly. His tongue flickered out over his fangs. "The master has waited long enough."

Just then the kitchen door banged open and Jake appeared holding a .38 revolver in his hands. Seeing Wanda's lifeless body on the floor, the mild-mannered cook was filled with righteous rage.

"You bastards!" He held the gun with both hands and fired point blank into the second vampire hitting him squarely in the chest with three rounds. The undead fiend was thrown off his feet into the coat rack by the door. He knocked over the wooden pole and steadied himself against the doorframe. Looking down at the holes in his coat, he shook his head and snarled like a vicious dog.

Before Jake could take a step back, the angry bloodsucker jumped him and together they disappeared through the kitchen portal. This was followed by the loud sounds of pots and pans clattering to the floor and then a piercing scream that was cut off suddenly.

At the same time Jazzy's mother sprang out of her seat grasping the porcelain plate on which her sandwiches had been delivered. Before the vampire could react, she whipped it around and smashed it into his face, her sandwich flying off in the opposite direction.

The strong plate shattered in her hands, shards cutting into the monster's dead flesh and breaking his nose. He growled and swiped at her with his long nails attempting to finish her as he had the helpless waitress. But the woman was faster and still holding the remaining piece of the smashed plate in her hand, she immediately drove it into the vampire's left eye with a powerful shove.

The monster bellowed and fell back from her.

Whereas Ravenwood was also backing up as he watched his opponent yank the rapier from his chest and toss it aside.

"Foolish mortal, I will make you suffer endlessly."

Ravenwood's right hand was behind his body groping for a particular object on the table. His fingers made contact and he clutched at the three-inch high glass container.

He whipped the saltshaker around, tore off the cap with his left hand and tossed its white granules into the vampire's descending mouth and face.

"You mean like this?"

The effect was instantaneous as the bits of salt bore into the vampire's flesh like tiny hot pokers; those in his mouth erupting into fiery spurts. His entire body was wracked with pain and began to shake violently as he attempted to wipe the burning pieces away and spit the others from his mouth. But it was too late and the fire inside his mouth seemed to flare brighter and burned his head from within. It burst into flames and he began spinning around wildly in the narrow aisle.

Ravenwood moved around the dancing, burning figure and bent to reclaim his rapier.

Meanwhile Jazzy's mother had taken a moment to turn her back on the vampire she had wounded to reach down and open her carry bag. She fumbled inside it and pulled out a foot-long gold crucifix that filled her hand and immediately held it out before her.

By now the crazed vampire had pulled the jagged piece of crockery from its ruined orb and was about to retaliate. At the sight of the cross, it screamed like a wild beast and put up its hands before its pale, gruesome face. It was in agony at the sight of the holy relic.

"Back you Satan spawned!" the brunette ordered, moving in closer.

Reluctantly the vampire shuffled back away from the offending cross.

"Jazzy, hurry!"

"Yes, mother."

The third undead by now had crumbled, burning away to ash before Ravenwood's startled eyes. So fast had his fiery consummation been that the white-hot flames hadn't lasted enough burn anything else in the confined space. Something the occult detective was grateful for.

He reached into his jacket and pulled his Luger from its under-the-arm holster and hurried to join the others in front of the door.

When the woman saw him over the shoulder of the vampire she was herding away from her and her daughter, she shook her head negatively. "Bullets cannot stop these....things."

Just then the kitchen door opened and the bloodied second vampire came rushing out.

Ravenwood twisted around and shot him in the head.

The monster stopped as it he had stuck a cement wall. His pink eyes rolled in their sockets and then he fell forward against the counter and was still.

The mysterious woman turned to Ravenwood who smiled, still holding tightly to his German made pistol. "I coat the bullets with Holy Water."

Then he shot the last vampire in the back of the head ending his threat forever.

"Who are you?" she asked puzzlement on her beautiful face. Her daughter remained hidden behind her.

"That's not important right now. Getting the two of you out here and to a safe place is. Will you trust me to do that?"

There was a moment's hesitation, then realizing she was still holding up her cross, she lowered her arm and said, "What other choice do we have? Lead on."

Ravenwood waited for her to retrieve her bag and then he opened the door and they stepped out into the night. He held his Luger at ready as he descended the three short steps to the pavement and pointed to the parked black convertible Alfa Romeo Spider Corsa in front of them. Its shiny surface reflected light spots from the nearby streetlamps. It was a small two-seater with the steering wheel on the right.

"But there's no room...?" the dark beauty said holding her daughter's arm with one hand and the heavy valise with the other.

Ravenwood dashed to the sleek sports car's rear and popped open the trunk. "Throw your bag in here. Jazzy will have to sit on your on your lap."

Just then there was a piercing howl and four dark clad shapes charged out of the alley across the street, their clawed hands reaching out; more vampires coming at them like a pack of ravenous wolves.

"HURRY!" Ravenwood stepped around the front of the Alpha Romeo and shot down two of the vampires in their tracks.

Before he could swing his aim to the third, the undead killer jumped over his head and landed on the Spider's rear cowling. Not seeing the older woman behind the upraised trunk, the monster sprang down onto Jazzy who barely had time to scream, "MOTHER!"

Transfixed by the sight of the high leaping vampire, Ravenwood had involuntarily taken his eyes off their fourth and last attacker. A second of distraction and suddenly he felt sharp nails digging into his arms as the monster was upon him, its fangs covered with drool, its awful fetid breath in his face. Holding his arms to his side in a superhuman grip, the hungry vampire lifted him off the ground. Its nails had penetrated the cloth of his coat and were digging deep into the flesh of his biceps.

He dropped the cane in his left hand but somehow willed himself to hold onto the Luger in his right, though there was no way he could ever bring it up in his current trapped state.

So be it.

Ravenwood twisted the automatic as best he could, imagining where the barrel was pointing and pulled the trigger.

His foe screamed and released him. It began jumping up and down on one foot, as it tried to hold up the foot he'd shot through with his tainted bullet. Dropping to the pavement, Ravenwood fired again at the creature, but because it was moving around so much his shot missed.

He remembered the two women and forgetting the wounded vampire, dashed around the small speedster in time to see Jazzy's mother come to her rescue.

The fiend atop the struggling teenager was pushing her hands down to clear an unobstructed path to her throat, its fangs exposed and eager to drink fresh blood. But it never got the chance as the enraged mother raced over and without hesitating kicked it in the side of the head with her pointed boot. The vampire fell over and onto its side. It tried to recover as Jazzy's mother stepped over her daughter to continue her assault on the unholy thing.

Unable to believe that a mere mortal woman was brave enough to confront it, the vampire sprang to its feet like a jumping jack, arms wide and ready. What it never saw coming was the ten-inch butcher's blade the woman suddenly withdrew from inside her cloak and the amazingly fast swing that cut off its head.

Dumbfounded by the woman's courage and lethalness, Ravenwood slammed the trunk lid closed and then went to help Jazzy get back on her feet.

"Your mother is a dangerous woman."

"You don't know the half of it," the girl said taking a deep breath.

"Save it for later." Ravenwood watched the woman kick the vampire's head down the sidewalk and approved. "Come on! Get in the car before any more of them show up!"

He put away his Luger, climbed into the car and kicked over the engine, setting his cane down beside him. As the racing engine roared to life, the woman ran around the front of the Spider, pulled open the door and fell back into the passenger seat while motioning her daughter to follow her.

At the same time the one-legged, hoping Vampire had stopped his crazy dance and was started to limp towards them.

The second Jazzy fell back onto her mother's lap, Ravenwood popped the clutch, pressed down on the gas pedal and the black Spider shot away down the road; the passenger door slamming shut with the forward motion.

Behind them the crippled vampire raised its arms toward the night sky and cried out in rage.

—✦—

"Your mother is a dangerous woman."

Baron Henri Savigne detested America with its New World opulence and upstart haughty airs as if it, by its very youth as a nation, was somehow better than the old world civilizations from which it had sprung. This condescending air of its people wherever he and his entourage traveled was offensive and continually fed his righteous indignation. Having to endure Americans and their uncivilized mannerism was perhaps the greatest challenge he had faced in well over three hundred years of existence; both as a human and now as one of the nosferatu.

In fact, the only thing of worth in the whole of this decadent metropolis they called New York was its abundance of fresh, wholesome blood; free for the taking.

As a Lord of the Imperial Vampire Court, he had smelled the ripe life-giving plasma coursing through the veins of the mindless human cattle all around him. How he yearned to unleash his bestial nature and feed freely on them as was his right. But the Court had made it quite clear that no such rampant blood shedding would be permitted during this hunt. Their mission was focused on one single objective, find the woman and her special child; capture them and return them to Paris. There they would be delivered to the Royal Court.

Looking about the dingy warehouse he had chosen as their base of operation, the ancient vampire could hear tramp steamers moving up and down the waterways of the Hudson River, their mournful whistles crying out in the night. At his feet, one of the two prostitutes he had fed on minutes earlier began to stir. Apparently he had not completely drained painted hussy as he had her companion. Baron Savigne signaled one of his minions, the burly Berleze, to come forth.

There was twelve of his undead troop, of both genders, scattered about the large, dank and cold warehouse. He commanded twice as many; the others were out scouring the night streets in search of their prey. He rotated them in shifts worried that too many on the loose simultaneously would invariably expose their presence and lead to disaster. He would not fail his superiors. Success could easily mean a place on the court for him when the time was right.

"Yes, my lord?" Berleze had been a miller from Belgium and somewhat dimwitted before having been turned. It annoyed the vampire leader to have to deal with him, but the brutish being's immense strength had increased ten-fold upon becoming one of the undead and thus he was a rare asset to the baron. Berleze's primary task was the protection of his master.

"Get rid of them," the baron commanded wiping his blood stained lips and chin with a silk handkerchief. "But be sure to take their off heads before you dispose of them.

"Do you understand?"

"Yes, master," the pale giant smiled grotesquely. "You do not want them to rise again."

"Indeed. The last thing we need is free agents running around attacking people and thus alerting the authorities to our presence in their midst."

Berleze reached down and picked up the groaning whore by the back of the neck. He broke it with a snap and then hoisted the body over his right shoulder. Effortlessly he picked up the remaining dead woman and set her on his left side before walking off towards the building's main double doors.

Another of the vampires, seeing Berleze marching by with his burden, raced over and pulled back one side of the portal only to jump back in surprise as a figure suddenly appeared from the dark outside.

"Gustof!" the would-be doorman mouthed, recognizing one of the six that had been dispatched earlier that evening.

Without acknowledging his fellow bloodsucker, Gustof pushed past him and moving with a very noticeable limp skirted around the big Berleze. By now all the lifeless eyes in the room were on the crippled vampire as he painfully marched up to his master where he came to a halt and bowed his head.

Baron Savigne, on his raised dais made from wooden pallets, looked down upon the one called Gustof. "Where are the others? And why are you limping?"

"We found them!" Gustof blurted, ignoring the questions put to them. "In a cheap diner near the theater district."

Savigne sat up straighter and leaned forward. "What? Are you sure?"

"Yes, my lord, it was them; the woman and her daughter. Their scent was unmistakable."

"Then where are they?" The vampire liege spread out his hands. "Why are they not here bound before me? And where are your cohorts. Tell me they have the bitch and her whelp and are now in the process of bringing them here."

At this Gustof seemed to shudder slightly. His pinkish eyes looked about furtively as all the others in the room had moved closer and were now encircling him, all as eager as their master to hear his words. Only the massive Berleze was absent, having simply continued on with his assignment as he was ordered. Even the sudden appearance of Gustof had not aroused the slightest iota of curiosity in the big vampire's mind. He only lived to obey his master.

"She escaped us…"

"WHAT!" The baron stood, anger shaping his face.

"….with the help of a stranger." Gustof clutched his hands together in front of his chest as if in prayer, shrinking in upon himself. "He had weapons…the bullets from his gun somehow manage to …to…"

"To what? Speak up you sniveling cur."

"They hurt …they could harm us…and did. With his help, they slew the others…all of them. Never to rise again."

There was a hushed murmur as the gathered vampires whispered amongst themselves at this incredible revelation.

"How is that even possible?' Baron Savigne stepped off his raised platform and stood before his frightened subject. "This stranger slew our brethren, left you wounded and then escaped with the countess and her child."

"Yes, my lord. That is what happened."

The vampire lord felt his anger rising and realized the folly of such a reaction. He could not afford the luxury of an uncontrollable rage.

Walking around the still worrisome Gustof, he motioned to several of the others. "Very, well, Gustof, I will accept your account, as ludicrous as it sounds. It only makes our task all the more difficult.

"We must learn the identity of this interloper and deal with him. But first I wish to examine these bullets with which he decimated six of my fellows."

At that the four vampires he had chosen stepped forward and took hold of Gustof and pulled him onto his back on the rough cement floor. He tried to fight them off, but it was useless.

"Remove his shoe." The baron raised his right hand the fingernails began to swell outward until they looked like talons. "Now, hold him steady while I retrieve this so-called…magic bullet."

It only took Ravenwood twenty minutes to drive to his apartment penthouse in the richest part of Manhattan. Going up the private elevator to his top floor suite, he was mildly amused at the young lift operator's reaction to his two guests. Sammy Edwards had been employed at the hotel for several years and had seen many strange types going up to Ravenwood's sanctum, but none as exotically beautiful as the dark haired woman or her cap-wearing teenage daughter.

They exited onto the fifth floor and entered a short hallway that led directly to the main entrance to his home. Ravenwood was carrying the woman's carpetbag in his free hand, his walking cane with the other.

"There are no other tenants?" asked the woman. She had remained stoically silence during the speedy ride from the diner.

"No," Ravenwood replied, slipping his key into the front door and opening it. "The entire floor is mine."

"And you live alone," she guessed walking past him as he swept his arm to invite the ladies into a lighted foyer.

"Hardly," he said, closing the door and then pressing an intercom button on the wall. "Sterling, we have guest. Meet us in my office."

There was a crackle from the speaker mesh and then a British voice was heard. "Yes, sir, at once."

With that, Ravenwood led the two women down a short corridor and into a large, ornately decorated room filled with bookshelves along the left and back walls. A massive wooden desk was set directly opposite the entrance and to their immediate right were fancy French doors covered with linen drapes. They opened onto a balcony with a spectacular view of the downtown. A fancy oriental rug covered the majority of the hardwood floor and to either side of it was a plush-looking sofa. Two leather clad chairs, both a russet brown faced the desk itself.

Ravenwood flicked the light switch and two standing lamps behind the sofas lighted the room. The room had an old-world feel to it and Jazzy was immediately taken with its atmosphere, especially the look of the rare tomes that filled the floor to ceiling bookshelves.

"Oh, mother, look," she exclaimed, moving along the wall, her finger touching the worn spines. "They are all about philosophy and magic."

Once again, Jazzy's mother turned her inquisitive green eyes to their host and repeated her earlier question. "Just exactly who are you and why are you armed as you are?"

"My name is Ravenwood, madam," he bowed slightly. "And I'm an investigator of the occult; thus my unusual weaponry. This was not my first encounter with the undead."

"Really." The woman bit her lower lip reflecting on his answer.

Just then Sterling, the tall, gray-haired butler, appeared behind them wearing a stylish robe over his black pajamas and wearing slippers. "Good evening, sir. Ladies."

"Ah, Sterling, there you are." Ravenwood smiled. "Please fix the guest bedroom, our guests will be spending the night."

"Very well sir. If the ladies wish, I can relieve them of their coats and hats."

Jazzy and her mother began removing their outer garments, relieved to be doing so while Ravenwood handed Sterling the heavy bag. "And after you've done, be so kind as to prepare a small repast for them. I know they have not dined this evening and must both be famished."

"Oh, no," the brunette said handing her hooded cloak to the waiting servant. Beneath she wore a simple, yellow cotton dress with short sleeves. "We don't want to put you to any more trouble."

"No trouble at all, Madam," the long faced Sterling declared. "It will only take me a few minutes to prepare a platter of cold meats and cheeses."

"That sounds great," Jazzy said holding her own coat and hat in her arms. "I'm really hungry, mother."

"Very well then. But why don't you accompany Mr. Sterling. He seems to have his hands full."

"Alright," the girl beamed, looking up at the stiff-necked Brit. "Hi, I'm Jazzy. Do have any peanut butter?"

Sterling crunched his face for a second before responding, "I do believe there is such an item in the food pantry. Come along, Miss ...ah...Jazzy. This way."

Ravenwood closed the door after them and invited Jazzy's mother to sit. She chose the nearest sofa as he went around his desk where he removed his jacket and draped it over the back of the swivel chair. He unfastened his shoulder holster with his Luger pistol and set it on the table next to a crystal decanter set.

"Would you join me in a brandy while we wait for Sterling to prepare your room?"

The woman arched her back and stretched her arms up over her head. "A brandy would be wonderful, Mr. Ravenwood. I confess, my nerves are rather frayed by what just happened."

As Ravenwood reached for the glass bottle, he heard the Nameless One's voice in his mind.

You brought her here! Into our sanctuary!

What was I supposed to do? Leave her and the child on the streets at the mercy of their foes?

There is an old spirit that surrounds her, my son. You must proceed with great care. This is like no other woman you have ever met.

Accepting his mentor's silent warning, the occult detective poured the ruby red liqueur into two small glasses. "From the conversation I overheard, you and Jazzy have been running from these creatures. Is that true?"

"It is," she sighed, dropping her arms and folding them under her bosom. "Ours is not a simple story."

He came over, handed her a glass and sat down at the other end of the settee. They both took a sip of the fiery elixir. Once more her radiant beauty was almost overpowering. Her alluring green eyes bore into him like those of a stalking tiger. "I assumed as much, madam....ah....perhaps we should start with your name."

"Dracula, sir. I am the Countess Marya Dracula, daughter of Count Vlad Dracula the Second of Wallachia. The one history has come to know as Vlad the Impaler."

━╱╲━

In his years as an occult detective, Ravenwood had heard many strange tales but none was as fantastic as that related to him by the mysterious dark haired beauty who now faced him.

"In the year 1412, hordes of Turks swept across the mid-eastern Romania's bent on the total conquest of the Christian Empire. My father, a knight in the Order of St. George, watched his armies slaughtered in battle after battle. The invading barbarians butchered the women folk of our homeland lamented in agony as fathers, sons, husbands and lovers and it appeared all was lost.

"Facing total defeat, seeing his people suffering, my father came to believe that God had abandoned him. In anger he lashed out at the church itself, publicly cursing the very cross he had once sworn to defend.

"During a particularly violent storm, my father walked across the last battlefield covered with the bodies of his men. In a passionate rage, he raised his gloved fists to the dark skies and there offered his allegiance to Satan and all his dark principalities if it would bring him victory and save his beloved Transylvania."

Marya took another sip of her brandy before continuing. "This part I'm afraid is hearsay, told to me by my father years later."

Ravenwood nodded. "Understood. Please continue."

"Apparently Lucifer heard my father's dire request for upon uttering it he was struck by lightning and hurled many yards into a lone standing tree. That he was not instantly killed was a sign that his petition had been granted. Rising to his feet, his armor smoking, Vlad Dracula was no longer human; he had become a vampire; one of the undead.

"What followed next is well documented in the history of our lands. Leading his remaining forces with his new, unholy powers, he became a true monster of death and destruction. When the Mongols discovered he could not be killed, they fled before him and Transylvania was saved.

"Racing to rejoin his family, my poor father was to learn there was yet another price to be paid for his pact with the devil. Before fleeing, a company of Mongols had attacked our castle and savagely butchered everyone within its walls.

"My mother and brothers were tortured and slain…all before my eyes…"

Tears began to slip down Marya's cheeks as she tried shaking loose the awful memories now resurfacing inside her. Ravenwood moved closer and put his hand over hers.

"How foolish of me," she apologized. "Tears are not something I easily shed, Mr. Ravenwood."

"Just Ravenwood, please. I take it you were not spared your own tribulations."

"That is putting it mildly. By the time my father and his men reached the castle, it was in ruins. And as you surmised, I too had been a victim of the Mongol's animal lust for vengeance and lay twisted and broken at the age of twelve before my father's tortured gaze. Heartbroken, he knelt and cradled me in his arms unwilling to lose me, the last of his children and so he did the only thing he could to save me; he gave me the kiss of the vampire.

"Yes, Ravenwood, I too would rise again and thus began our journey together through time as the last of the Draculas. The invasion quelled, the people of the surrounding villages pledged themselves to us in gratitude for what my father had done. They vowed to serve us faithfully as long as we continued to walk the earth.

"For the next four hundred years, we existed in the seclusion of our ancestral home, feeding off the blood of the living. I am sorry if this repulses you."

Both of them drained their glasses and Ravenwood took her empty glass. "I'll wait until I've heard the entire tale before judging you, countess."

"Marya, please. The old ways are ghosts in this new modern age."

"You say you were turned at the age of twelve," Ravenwood pointed out as he stood and brought the glasses back to his desk. "It is obvious that even as a vampire, you continued to mature."

"Yes, I did. Somewhere in my twenty-fifth year I ceased aging completely. And as long as I continued to feed, maintained my youth and supernatural vigor."

Ravenwood returned to the sofa and sitting, smiled awkwardly. "And still it is obvious you have aged still further."

Marya Dracula brought her left hand up to her black hair with its few strands of gray and returned his smile. "You are gallant, sir. Yes, at present I am ….well, let us say, I am now aging as any other woman does."

This brought a puzzled expression to his face and Marya went on with her story.

"Eventually my father could no longer withstand our confinement and dared to begin traveling abroad until he found himself in Great Britain where he met a young lady who bore a striking resemblance to my mother. Blinded by her appearance, he became reckless and his true nature was revealed. Thus he was trapped and finally put to death forever.

"You can well imagine my sorrow when I learned of his fate. For the first time since all these horrific events had begun; I was truly alone in the world. Back then, I had no inkling there were others such as I; something I would only discover much later to my misfortune. In the meanwhile, I resigned myself to my solitary existence. My only social interaction was with those villagers who continued to fill the ranks of the castle's staff from one generation to the next. They, and the wretched victims they would procure for me in their devotion to their ages old pledge.

"Thus my cursed existence until the eve of the Great War when it seemed the whole world had gone crazy. Then a chance meeting on the grounds of our estate began a chain of events that would alter my future and prove to be the salvation of my soul. I met a young German lad named Manfred von Richthofen."

"The bloody Red Baron was your father!" Sterling almost dropped the pitcher of milk in his hands at Jazzy's proclamation of her lineage. They were in the large, spotlessly clean kitchen. She was seated at the table spreading huge gobs of peanut butter on slices of French bread while Ravenwood's butler was about to pour her a glass of milk before he cut up cheese and cold meats for her mother and his employer.

"Hmm…hmmm," she mumbled chewing on the delicious spread.

"Mother said they met just before the war started and she fell in love with him the second she met him. Enough so that she traveled the Berlin years later to find him again."

Sterling poured the milk while his thoughts went back in time. "Amazing, truly amazing. You see, I was a pilot myself, Miss Jazzy, in the Royal Air Force. I flew in many aerial duels over the ravaged landscapes of France and Germany."

"You mean dogfights." She swallowed a mouthful while reaching for the cold white milk. She took a long drink. Wiping her mouth with a napkin, she asked, "Did you ever see my father? Mother says his Fokker was painted a very bright red."

"Indeed it was," Sterling confirmed. "But I had the good fortune to never see it personally. Had I done so, I might not be here today. Your father was one of the greatest aces to ever take to the skies.

"I remember when we received word that he had been shot down..." Sterling realized the words coming from his mouth and looked at the bright-eyed young girl with apprehension. "Oh...forgive me..."

"It's okay, really." Jazzy dug into the jar of peanut butter with the butter knife he had given her. "I never really knew him. He died before I was even born." She smeared the brown goop on another slice of bread. "To me he's just a story."

Sterling went to the icebox to fetch the cheese and salami roll. "Still, you should be proud of your heritage, Miss Jazzy. He was truly a remarkable, brave man."

"I suppose." She started nibbling on her treat. "Still, the greatest thing he really did was stop mother from being a vampire."

Sterling dropped the block of cheese.

➤⟋⟍➤

"You can imagine my insane rage upon learning of Manny's death," Marya continued her incredible tale. "Hell hath no fury as woman scorned, I believe is how the Bard put it."

"But by then you were pregnant with Jazzy?"

"I was...but I didn't know it yet. I was filled with an all-consuming hatred for the Allied fliers who had taken my love from me. Manfred had wiped out five hundred years of loneliness with his caresses and then, in a cruel twist of fate, he was taken from me.

"The weeks following his death were a blur. I used all of my dark powers to lay waste to Allied squadrons and commanded thousands of rats to swarm over their airdromes. My need for revenge blinded me to all else.

"And then, one morning, returning to the safety of Castle Dracula before the sun's rise, I collapsed in excruciating pain before my servant, Irena; an old woman who had been with me for many years. I vomited blood, so much.....it just spewed out of me as if my body could not longer accept it."

"Something that had never happened before." Ravenwood could sense the weariness in Marya and that she was coming to climax of her story.

"Of course not. I was a vampire. Human blood was what sustained me. Why should I now suddenly be unable to digest it? Of course it was wise Irena who guessed the answer."

"You were pregnant with Jazzy."

"Yes, as impossible as that was for me to believe. How could something alive take seed in something foul and undead such as I?

"Irena argued that it was Manfred's true love that had brought about this miracle and if in fact I could no longer drink the blood of others, then it meant the curse of my vampirism had been lifted; that I was once again mortal.

"But how could I be certain? How could I be absolutely sure I was no longer one of the undead, that the Almighty in his infinite mercy had forgiven me? Of course the answer was simple enough. All I had to do was leave the darkness interior of the castle and venture forth into the sunlight of the new day exposing myself to a sun I had not beheld in over five hundred years."

At this point Marya took a deep breath and exhaled it slowly.

"I take it you survived the test."

She looked at him and nodded. "It is a moment I shall never forget, Ravenwood, as long as I have left in this world. To walk out on that parapet overlooking our vast estate and feel the warm rays of the sun bathe my flesh in a euphoric baptism of redemption.

"I fell to my knees, clasped my hands together in prayer and gave thanks to a truly loving God who does forgive beyond our imagination.

"The rest all happened swiftly enough. I had the castle boarded up and left it to begin my...*our* new life. I traveled to Belgium and there gave birth to Jazemara and remained there for several years. Keep in mind, our family's wealth was hidden away in banks across Europe and my daughter and I wanted for nothing.

"Those were glorious, happy years. As Jazemara grew...so did I, like any normal woman should. But I was no longer afraid of the process or the fact that one day I too would pass from this reality into the next. Having been granted so powerful a miracle, I was truly humbled and daily appreciative of the truest treasure this world has to offer, love."

Marya paused then as if reliving every memory just as she had related them. In the quiet between them Ravenwood could not help but believe her sincerity. As outrageous as the tale appeared, he believed every word of it.

As you should, my son. The Nameless One's mental confirmation was tremendously assuring. Ravenwood had been well aware his old mentor had been listening to the woman's account through his eyes. Something he was skilled at doing.

Everything she has said is the truth. But as before, she and the girl are still in grave danger and it will be your decision as to whether to send them or their way or become involved with their plight.

But father, I could only act as you've taught me. In his mind he saw the Nameless One's tiny smile. He'd given him the right answer.

"Alright, Marya," he broke the mental contact. "Who are these vampires chasing you and Jazzy?"

Before Dracula's daughter could answer that question, Sterling reappeared pushing a cart on which was a silver platter filled with cheeses and meat and a carafe of coffee surrounded by porcelain cups. Jazzy waltzed in behind him holding a large mug of hot cocoa.

Sterling brought the wheeled cart to the center of the room, put his arms behind his back and asked, "Will this do, sir?"

As the amiable Sterling set about feeding his employer and his guests, the Nameless One sat cross-legged on his padded floor mat in his small, square room. Situated in the exact center of the penthouse, it was the only room without any windows and the old man preferred it as such. The only furniture in the room was a wooden bed against one wall and a tiny wooden altar against the back wall opposite the single door. On this rested an ivory sculptured statue of the Buddha. On either side of the figure were two scented candles that filled the tiny room with a pleasant, woodsy smell. The room was equipped with electricity and an overhead light was affixed to the ceiling but the Nameless One never used it, the noise of the speeding electrons disturbed his meditation.

His old mentor had been listening to the woman's account through his eyes.

Now, seated on the floor before the white Buddha, he began to slow his breathing and enter into a deep meditative state. He was a small figure, his aged body virtually devoid of any excess fat, his thin limbs tough, his weathered skin tanned almost bronze. He wore his pale white hair shoulder length and a thin gossamer-like beard fell to his chest. He was dressed in gray cotton pants and a matching button-less tunic.

As he began humming the holy Tibetan mantras he had been taught as a child, he unconsciously ran his bony fingers through his beard, a habit he had developed to soothe his always-curious mind and allow him to draw deep within his own soul. His eyes closed welcoming the dark warmth of the universe around him and he continued to hum, his breathing lessening with each rhythmic beat of his powerful heart. Deeper he fell into his own being until a light appeared before him. He sent his true astral body after it.

Just like that he was floating in the air before his physical body; an experience he had undergone more times than he could remember. He prepared to fly out and find those agents of evil that threatened his adoptive son.

His invisible specter glided through the walls of his room, down the corridor and into Ravenwood's office where the others were gathered. The woman with the black hair was conversing while pausing every few minutes to partake of the nourishment the butler had delivered. Though old beyond reckoning, the Nameless One could still appreciate true beauty when he beheld it and at seeing Marya Dracula he understood why his American son was smitten with her. At the same time the daughter's aura was charged with a golden energy and the Nameless One saw in her a powerful spirit capable of much potential if she were protected and kept from the clutches of those who hunted them.

Father? Ravenwood had sensed his astral presence but didn't let on to the others, continuing to be an attentive host while aware of his nearness.

I go to find the evil ones and their nest. Remain vigilant. When I return, I will call you and the countess to my room.

As you wish, Old One.

And with that the one time Tibetan monk floated up through the ceiling, through the buildings roof and out into the skies over Manhattan.

For any lesser spirit, the task before him would have been hopeless. Manhattan was the home to millions, each emanating a spiritual light. A lesser Yogi would have been unable to discern individual souls amidst this mighty assemblage, their *chis* merging together in a swirling whirlpool of humanity. But Tibetan monks who were masters of astral projection had taught the Nameless One and his ability to differentiate amongst the multitude below him was his true power.

The sky over the city was a blue-black canvas. In the distance, beyond the harbor were small flashes of lightning and he could feel the moisture in the molecules around him. A storm was coming and with it rain. As he flew over the buildings and streets below, the Nameless One made no effort to guide his essence in any particular direction. All the while his soul continued to receive impressions from the ether, signals from the populace beneath him. Thoughts of decency, charity, love as well as those of cruelty, sadism and pure selfishness. All washed through him as he floated freely through the cloudless heavens.

He was looking down at the Hudson River when the odorous wave of occult bestiality assaulted him. So strong was its essence he was nearly shaken from his self-induced trance and hurled back into his physical shell; still at rest back in his room. Girthing his mental shield, the Nameless One followed the evil essence downward to its source and he found himself hovering above a squat, broken down warehouse abutting the piers of an abandoned dock site. As he descended lower to the roof the stench of the undead permeated him completely.

This was it; the secret enclave of the foreign vampires. No sooner had that thought arisen in his consciousness then he saw several scurrying figures appear from the alley beside the warehouse. Moving more like animals than people, the Nameless One watched the vampires hurry to the warehouse's front entrance and slip inside. He could make out the street number over the sliding doors.

It was enough. To go any further might alert the foul things as their own supernatural abilities were many. No, he had achieved his goal. Lifting his arms wide, the Nameless One rose into the air as thunder rolled in from the shores of New Jersey.

He opened his eyes….and was back in his room.

"When Jazemara was six, we left Belgium for Paris," Marya Dracula related as she put down her empty coffee cup. "I wanted her to have a broad education; to be familiar with various world cultures and such. Paris was such a cosmopolitan atmosphere."

Ravenwood nodded as Jazzy made a face to let her mother know for the millionth time how much she did not like her own name. It was so old fashioned. Meanwhile, Sterling sat on the opposite sofa, awaiting any further instructions. His hastily put-together repast has been well picked over by their lovely guest and now Marya was finishing the story of their ordeal.

"It truly is a wonderfully city," Ravenwood concurred. "I was happy to learn it had not suffered any great damage from the war."

"Oh, no, it is very much the center of the new bohemian movement," Marya continued. "What with artists and poets from around Europe gathering there to create a brand renaissance." She sighed. "The very thing to attract those who dwell in the shadows.

"You see, it was there that we were approached by agents of the Imperial Vampire Court. Although I had vague memories of my father having mentioned we were not the only ones of our kind, his words had long since faded from my thoughts and in my naiveté at being cured, I foolishly ignored the possibilities that other such....creatures still walked amongst the dark alleys of world.

"You can imagine my surprise when I was visited one night by two gentlemen in fancy clothing identifying themselves as vampires sent by this so-called Court to contact me in regards to Jazemara's lineage and her supposed destiny."

"How so?" Ravenwood started to get up, his own cup empty. Sterling, ever watchful, jumped to his feet, took the mug and refilled it without spilling a drop.

"Thank you, Sterling." The butler nodded and returned to his place on the long sofa.

"They want me to be their new Queen of the Vampires," Jazzy blurted out, seeing the pause in her mother's explanation. "All because I'm Dracula's granddaughter."

"Jazemara, please do not interrupt me."

"Sorry. But it's true."

"Yes, my dear. That was the purpose of their visit." Marya looked at Ravenwood, her green eyes imploring him to understand her fears. "Somehow this group of elite vampires had learned of Jazemara's birth and saw it as some kind of a sign—that she should become their queen."

"But she isn't even a vampire?" Sterling said caught up in the story. "Ah… is she?"

He turned his gaze to Jazzy who immediately stuck out her tongue at him.

"Of course not, Mr. Sterling. Jazemara was conceived in true, pure love. A love so powerful it cleansed my own soul and she has never once exhibited the slightest hint of that foul tainting."

"Then for her to assume this role she would have to be turned," Ravenwood finished for Marya.

"Something that will never happen as long as I live," Marya's words were hard edged. "Knowing how precarious our position was, in a strange city with no real allies, I lied and told them their proposal was something I needed time to consider…that maybe, instead of Jazemara, I could once again join their ranks and assume that role.

"My words seemed to placate them and they departed saying they would return within a week for my answer. I realized our only recourse was to leave Paris and that very night I packed what few belongings we had and we fled."

"Where did you go?"

"England. It was but a short journey across the channel and once there, we took up residency in a small hamlet on the coast of Wales far from the major populace centers such as London or Manchester. I prayed we had successfully eluded them and for the next few years we did. But they are relentless, if nothing else, and eventually tracked us down. Once again we fled. This time across the ocean to Canada where we lived until a few months ago."

"Where they found you again." Ravenwood found the vampires' obsession formidable indeed. If they were willing to chase half way around the world for Marya and her daughter, what could possibly stop them?

"Yes. They attacked us one evening as I was picking her up from a school dance. I was just barely able to fend them off long enough for us to reach the train station and book passage south. That was three days ago, Ravenwood. We haven't stopped running since."

"Then," said a very soft voice, "perhaps it is time you did so, dear lady."

All eyes turned to the open doorway where the old man in the gray clothing stood, his arms folded casually behind his back. Sterling nearly fell off the sofa, so rare were the times when the Nameless One ventured outside his room.

Ravenwood had almost the same reaction, rising to his feet and greeting his revered mentor. "Father. Let me introduce you to our guests; the Countess Marya Dracula and her daughter, Jazemara."

The Nameless One bowed slightly and then grinned at the teenage girl. "I trust your mother will forgive me," he said. "But I too like Jazzy much better."

Having put them at ease, the Nameless One turned to the butler. "It has been a long night. Could I possibly trouble you for a cup of herbal tea?"

"I suppose I can find something in the pantry." Sterling rose with a huff and exited the room.

Marya, sensing his ire, turned to Ravenwood who merely shrugged. "Cats and dogs, they are like this all the time."

"My intention was not to annoy your servant, my son. But rather, I believe I have the answer to the countess' situation. One that will effectively end the threat of the Vampire Court to her and Jazzy forever."

"How could you do that?" Marya asked surprised by the old man's claim.

"Well, in two ways, dear lady. The first is to effectively eliminate the present threat to you here in this place."

"And the second?"

"To deliver you and Mistress Jazzy to a place no evil can ever find you again."

Inspector Horatio Stagg marched up and down the sidewalk in front of the abandoned waterfront warehouse like a frustrated marionette on strings. He was a short, chunky man with deep set eyes and reminded people of a human bulldog with his brown derby and rumpled corduroy suit of the same color. His officers respected him as a by-the-book honest cop who never shirked his duties. Inspector Stagg would never ask any of them to do anything he would not do himself.

Which was why twelve of them, in their dark blue uniforms, were gathered together in front of four parked radio cars awaiting his orders. Waiting to learn why they had been ordered to this river dockside as a glaring yellow sunrise splashed across the skies behind them. There was a predawn chill in the air signifying that autumn wasn't too far off. All around them were stevedores arriving for work to unload the giant ships waiting at anchor to divest themselves of their various cargoes.

Stagg and his men had arrived fifteen minutes earlier as directed by Ravenwood. Although the inspector was a skeptic and didn't believe in all the supernatural mumbo-jumbo that was Ravenwood's stock and trade, he couldn't deny the man had helped him on several occasions when certain cases involved bizarre, unexplained phenomena. In his cop's heart, he knew it was all a con, tricks to pull the wool over gullible civilians. But not him, no sirree. Horatio Stagg knew better.

Which only infuriated him more. Here he was with his men wasting time all because of a midnight phone call from Ravenwood requesting his help. When Stagg had asked for specifics, the eccentric investigator had replied vaguely about some nest of monsters threatening the city. Monsters! Really!

Stagg started to reach into his jacket pocket to grab a handful of roasted peanuts from the paper bag he always carried when the sound of a sports car turned his attention to the corner. Ravenwood's sleek black Alfa Romeo Spider Corsa appeared and speeded to where the police vehicles were parked. It came to a smooth stop and Stagg hurried over as the engine died and Ravenwood, looking tired, climbed out. At the same time a tall, striking woman emerged from the passenger side wearing a hooded cloak. Giving her a cursory glimpse, the veteran cop greeted the Stepson of Mystery in his usual manner.

"Alright, fancy pants, what the hell is going on that necessitated you dragging me and my men out here at the bloody crack of dawn?"

"Good morning to you as well, Inspector," Ravenwood maintained a straight face as he turned and walked to the rear of his automobile. "I am most grateful for your willingness to meet us here. Allow me to open the trunk and I'll explain what we are all doing here."

As Ravenwood unlocked the boot and raised the cover, Marya came to stand by his side. In the trunk was a huge canvas bag, which the occult detective opened wide for Stagg to inspect.

In it were dozens of wooden stakes, each a foot long, four heavy mallets, some machetes and several silver flasks filled with Holy Water.

"What the hell is all this for?" Stagg asked picking up one of the big mallets and several stakes. "You hunting vampires now?"

Despite himself, Ravenwood smiled. "Inspector Stagg, you never fail to astound me with your honed deductive skills. That is exactly what we are here for." He moved around the inspector and pointed to the warehouse. "We will find them hidden inside. Most likely resting in their coffins now that the sun has risen. It is the time they are the most vulnerable."

Stagg stood with his mouth agape. By now several of his men had come closer and heard Ravenwood's declaration. All their eyes were on their leader.

Stagg blinked and then started to laugh, tossing the mallet and stakes back into the trunk. "Jesus, Mary, Joseph, Ravenwood, you've finally gone completely bonkers. Vampires!! God…if that ain't the funniest thing…"

Marya stepped up behind the ranting copper and grabbed him by the back of the neck. With one hand she lifted him off his feet. He yelled in surprise, his feet kicking in the air, his eyes frantically trying to look back at who it was holding him so easily.

"You think vampires are amusing?" Marya snarled. "I assure you, sir, they are not. They are real predators who will inflict great harm unless you aid us in destroying them here and now."

"Geezus…lady…put me down!"

Marya complied none too gently. Stagg stumbled and put out a hand to steady himself. Then, catching his breath, spun around to face the countess. "How the hell did you do that?"

"I was once a vampire. The strength it took to pick you up just now is but a small example of the powers I once possessed. Powers wielded by all the foul things hiding in that building at this very moment.

"Vampires are real, inspector. Ignore that and the horrors that will follow will be on your head."

Horatio Stagg swallowed hard. As much as he was angry for being publicly humiliated in front of his men, the grim look in Marya's eyes gave him pause. *What if she and Ravenwood were telling the truth? A vampire scourge on Manhattan!* A sick look came over his face. What other choice did he have? If Ravenwood was crazy, they'd break into the warehouse, find it empty and then he could lock him up, and the crazy strong dame, for any number of minor misdemeanors. On the other hand if they were legit…

"Alright," he muttered, turning back to Ravenwood. "But if all this is some kind of hoax, I'll lock you away so fast, you won't know what hit you."

"Fair enough, Inspector." Ravenwood nodded towards the trunk. "Can we proceed now?"

Stagg pointed to two of the nearest policemen. "Carter and Monroe, you two grab that duffel bag inside the trunk and follow us. The rest of you draw your guns and be ready for anything." At that the boys in blue unholstered their revolvers except for the two men assigned to carry the heavy canvas bag.

Seeing this, Ravenwood and Marya started up the cement steps leading to the platform and the twin sliding doors that opened into the warehouse. Stagg was immediately behind them, his own .38 clutched in his right hand.

There was no lock of any kind on either door and the veteran detective pushed past Ravenwood, grabbed a wooden handle and pulled it sideways. It made very little noise as it slid away on steel rollers leaving them facing the darkened interior.

The harsh light of the new day fell over their shoulders, its presence a comforting element as they eyed the stygian blackness that awaited them inside the massive, empty building.

Not one to hesitate, Inspector Horatio Stagg marched forward into what appeared to be a wide-open space. The cement floor was covered with a thick layer of dust now being kicked up by his footfalls. There was a dim light from high over head and he looked up to see long, tall windows that had been covered by a thick green paint, still they could not completely blot out the outdoor light.

Ravenwood and Marya flanked him to either side, both moving just cautiously as their eyes gradually adjusted to the gloomy interior. The place reminded Stagg of an empty church being so vast and spread out. He would not have minded a few candles here and there. His shoes stepped on something brittle and he stopped to look down. Reaching into his coat pocket he pulled out a wooden match and lit it by scratching it with his thumbnail. Immediately the robust flame illuminated his torso.

"What?" Ravenwood turned to him.

"I'm stepping on something weird." Stagg bent over slightly with the burning match and revealed the carcasses of dozens of dead rats and mice. "Sweet Jesus! What the hell?"

"Seems our friends were snacking," Ravenwood suggested wryly.

Before the light burned out, one of the uniformed men behind them called out. "Over there, up ahead. Are those crates?"

The group moved forward until the shapes became familiar pieces of furniture; a few desks covered with paper litter and a half dozen wooden chairs fallen over. Stagg lit another match and was pleasantly surprised to find several candles scattered amidst the clutter on the desktops. He picked one up and hurriedly lit the wick tip before his match went out.

"Some of you guys light those other candles," he directed.

Soon four candles were aglow and the visible area around them began to widen. Marya, whose eyes were the keenest, spotted what they were searching for beyond the abandoned office equipment. "Over there," she said pointing, "along that back wall."

Ravenwood and Stagg, who was still holding his candle, walked around the desks spreading the yellow glow even further; enough to recognize the cheap wooden coffins covering the floor before them.

"Holy crap!" Stagg gasped. "How many of them are there?" he asked while mentally trying to count.

"Eighteen," Ravenwood replied. "There are eighteen of them, Inspector. I suggest we start from the closest to us and work our way to the wall. That way, if any of them become …active…we'll be able to herd them in and cut off any means of escape they may have."

"What the hell do you mean by…active?"

It was Marya who explained further. "They are not sleeping, inspector. The undead can never really sleep. They rest now, unable to face the rays of the sun. So, even though they are weakened and vulnerable, in such a darkened place they might still have enough strength to react; to fight. None of your men must hesitate to do what must be done. Do you understand me?"

"I think so, lady." Stagg tilted his round derby back on his head. "But why don't you and Ravenwood here demonstrate it for us. That way there won't be any screw ups."

"Very well," Ravenwood agreed. By now officers Carter and Monroe had set the bag of instruments on one of the dirty desks. He went to it, rummaged through it and pulled out a mallet, several wooden stakes and a flask.

Returning to Marya, he handed her the silver flask while addressing Stagg. "Stay close to me with that candle." Then he looked over the inspector's shoulder at the anxious faces watching them. "You others grab tools and gather around, but not too closely and stay alert. This is going to be most unpleasant."

With that he walked over to the nearest coffin and knelt down on one knee beside it. Stagg stood behind him holding up the candle while Marya took a spot at the top of the long box and uncapped the flask in her hand.

She looked down at Ravenwood. "Ready when you are."

Without further preamble, the occult detective slammed the mallet upward along the side of the coffin catching the lip of the cover. It ripped up in one piece and fell to the floor opposite him. Inside was a female vampire dressed in moldy clothing and reeking of rotten meat, her colorless face smeared with pieces of vermin blood and gore.

Ravenwood leaned over and placed the sharpened tip of his wooden stake against her chest and began to raise the mallet over his head. Suddenly the vampire's dull red eyes opened and she snarled at the sight of him. She began to rise up only to have Marya lean over and spill Holy Water onto her face. It sizzled upon contact and the undead creature screamed in pain, her clawed hands going to her damaged face.

"Ready when you are."

It was all the diversion the Stepson of Mystery required as he slammed his hammer down with all his might and drove the stake into her heart. Blood bubbled up from the wound like a tiny geyser and the foul creature's body convulsed violently. Her hands tried to pull at the offending steak at which point, Marya reached into her cloak and brought forth her butcher's blade. With one powerful stroke she cleaved the vampire's head off its neck. The creature stopped moving…in true death.

Ravenwood reached in, took hold of the now lifeless monster's head by her hair and standing, held it aloft for all to see. "Make sure to remove their heads. It is the only sure way to guarantee they will never rise again." He then tossed it away to land with a plop yards away.

At the exact same time several of the coffins began to rattle as if something inside them was moving.

"They know we are here," Marya warned. "There is no time to waste."

"Yah heard the lady," Stagg growled. "Form up into pairs and get busy. All of you." The nearest coppers stood transfixed, some still staring at the headless body with the stake in its chest. "NOW!!!" Bellowed Stagg. "What dah hell do you think this is; a picnic?"

Jumping, the officers shook off their fears and began opening coffins.

"Come on," Stagg said to Ravenwood as he started towards another rattling coffin. "Let's get this freaking job over with."

Fifty feet away, hidden in an expediter's backroom alcove, Baron Henri Savigne heard the screams of his ghoulish pack and immediately knew they were under attack. He pushed up the cover to his more lavish coffin and sat up. Like all such mobile repositories, the satin cushions beneath him were covered with dirt from his French hometown. Quickly he climbed out and whipped his black cape about his shoulders. The noises from within the warehouse were growing louder. He could hear hammers pounding into cold flesh, the agonized screams of his children as they were set upon by unknown forces.

He moved through the darkness to a second, much larger coffin, set beside the room's single door. He hurriedly pried it open to reveal his loyal servant, Berleze.

"Get up," he whispered. "And be quiet. We are under attack."

Clumsily the big vampire pulled himself from his own crate-sized coffin just as there was a chorus off shouts coming from the main hall.

Both recognized them as human cries. They were followed by two loud gunshots.

Baron Savigne carefully opened the door and exited. To his right was the back door to the loading docks and back alleys. To his left was the warehouse itself and pressing himself against the wall he saw policemen moving about the coffins of his people like eerie death-dealing specters in the harsh flickering light of the moving candles.

But how had the authorities found them?

Then, as the light continued to move about he recognized the person with the hooded cloak. It was a woman…the woman! The countess herself! So that was how the police had found them out. The bitch had turned the tables on her hunters. She was as ruthless as she was clever, he mused. But now it became a matter of survival. There was no way he, even with Berleze's strength, could overcome that many hunters.

They had only one recourse; to find shelter. And they had to go now before they were discovered!

━╱╲━

Ravenwood held his Luger by his side ready for any other struggling vampires. The police had begun their work of destroying the odious beings and the first few went well enough. But when one pair opened the fifth coffin, the ravenous vampire inside lunged up at them before they could act. With frantic desperation he'd knocked down the officer with the mallet and stake and then sprung up out of the box and struck at the second man with his long sharpened nails. The cop's cheek was cut open and he fell back dropping his flask of Holy Water.

Like a maddened clown, the freed vampire had cackled and turned around eyeing its foes, hands out ready to wreak more destruction. Ravenwood had immediately dropped his own tools and rushed to confront the crazed killer. He had drawn his pistol from its shoulder rig and shot the thing in the head…twice. It collapsed in front of the two shaken coppers.

"See why you have to work fast," he reminded them holding his gun up. "Somebody help that officer and get those cuts on his face seen to. The rest of you keep at it!"

All of that had transpired in a less than a minute. Now the occult detective stood ready to assist any of the other teams should another bloodsucker prove too difficult to vanquish.

"Ravenwood!" Marya came up behind him and grabbed his elbow.

"What?"

"I thought a heard a door open and close back there, towards the rear of the building."

He looked over and could just make out the outlines of a door. "Are you sure?"

"Yes," she said clutching his arm. "Right after you fired your pistol. I think some of them may have escaped."

Seeing the worry on her face, Ravenwood had no choice but to believe her. He saw Stagg working with a pair of officers to open another coffin closer to the back wall and called out to him. "Stagg, some may have gotten out the back. We're going to check it out. You and your men keep at it."

The short inspector merely waved to him in acknowledgement as Ravenwood and Marya ran to the back of the building.

He was the first to reach the door and pulling it open was temporarily blinded by sunshine. He blinked several times and was stunned to see two figures hurrying down the middle of the alleyway. One was massive while the other was wrapped in a thick cape. Both of them were aflame as a gray smoke exuded from their bodies and their progress was clearly awkward and difficult.

"Dear God," Marya exclaimed as she came alongside of him and sighted the fleeing vampires. "Where are they running to? There is nowhere for them to hide."

But Marya was wrong. Ravenwood spotted the circular outline of a manhole cover in the middle of the street. That was obviously their goal; to get into the sewers away from the burning sun and then evade their pursuers.

Ravenwood fired at them but missed. Neither vampire looked back as both were totally focused on the round, heavy steel plate. Reaching it, the smaller of the two, turned and directed the big one to lift it up. In doing so his head was visible to Marya and she recognized him immediately.

"Baron Savigne! He was one of the men who approached us in Paris."

Despite the awful pain he was suffering, Berleze squeezed his fingers under the edge of the manhole lid and easily tore off the gaping hole beneath. Ravenwood fired again and hit the undead behemoth in the back. Grunting in pain, Berleze spun about and with a mighty heave hurled the manhole cover.

It spun through the air like a top straight for Ravenwood and Marya. Ravenwood tackled her to the pavement seconds before the deadly disc flew by. It crashed into a pile of old trashcans, mashing them as if they were made of cardboard.

On the ground, Ravenwood dared lift his head just in time to see the baron starting to drop into the sewer opening. He looked back at them, his face bubbling red and yelled up at the big vampire, "STOP THEM!"

"Yes, master." Berleze began to shamble towards Ravenwood and Marya. The unbearable heat was causing his entire body to combust with each stumbling step he took. But his dimwitted mind refused to accept his fate in carrying out his master's order.

Ravenwood, still prone on the rough tar of the alleyway pointed his Luger at the oncoming mass of fiery hell and fired three more rounds into it with seemingly no effect. Then, only a few yards from them, the monster staggered, raised its arms skyward and cried out in anguished doom before crashing down. Its entire body burst asunder becoming nothing but black ash and skeletal pieces within seconds. A gust of wind blew over the remains as the flames died out and all that was left of Berleze were his bones and smoldering tatters of his clothes.

Warily Ravenwood put away his gun and got to his feet at the same time helping Marya up. Together they approached the smoking shape.

"Give me your knife," Ravenwood said and Marya handed it over. With a fast stroke, the Stepson of Mystery detached the skull from the corpse and then kicked it down the alley. That done, the two of them approached the open manhole and peered down into its dark well.

"We have to go after him," Marya urged.

"I know. But we need a light. Or else we'll be sitting ducks down there."

"There's no time."

Ravenwood looked at the long, fat butcher's blade in his hand. "Then we'll have to improvise."

He raised the sharp cutting weapon and carefully put both his hands to either side of the clean, shiny blade. Then he closed his eyes and began to utter a Tibetan magic spell he had learned from the Nameless One. His voice was low as he softly repeated the foreign words over and over in a practiced cadence.

After a few seconds, the blade began to glow as if it held some inner electrical charge.

Marya's eyes widened in awe at what she was seeing. There was much more to her new ally than she had suspected.

Ravenwood opened his eyes to a glimmering blade as bright as any torch.

"Now we're ready." Marya nodded. "Stay close to me."

"Yes, but please, Ravenwood, let's hurry."

Ravenwood gave her the glowing knife and started to climb down the rusty ladder just inside the manhole opening. At chest level he opened his hand and she once again passed the deadly weapon to him and he descended completely out of sight.

Steadying her resolve with a deep breath, Marya removed her cumbersome cloak, tossed it aside and began down the ladder into the black depths below.

⟶ 〟〵 ⟵

Ravenwood stepped off the last rung of the ladder into fetid water that reached to his ankles—so much for his expensive Italian shoes. As Marya climbed down, he moved away from the ladder into the inky blackness around them, his feet making sloshing noises. The glowing butcher's cleaver illuminated the red brick walls that made up the long narrow tunnel that ran into two different directions from the manhole entrance. The air was both cool and foul, the water a sickly brown color.

"Be careful," he whispered as he used his free hand to assist Marya's last few downward steps. "There is water here and the floor beneath is slick."

The lovely brunette stepped down carefully holding on to his forearm. "Lovely. I wasn't expecting a tour of the city's nether regions." She wrinkled her nose. "And that smell is overripe as well."

"Methane," Ravenwood said. "It's a good thing we didn't bring in any candles. The gas is dangerously flammable."

Marya released his arm and put her index up over her lush lips to quiet him. She titled her head and listened. Ravenwood couldn't hear at thing. Then he too heard a splashing sound coming from the tunnel to their right.

"Yes," Marya softly agreed. "That way."

Taking the lead, his glowing knife before him, Ravenwood began moving down the waterway. As he walked, doing his best to minimize the noise of the water sucking at his feet, he recalled the history of the city's underground passages. Most of the current sewage tunnels had been constructed after the Civil War by returning veterans as the great urban metropolis' population continued to grow with the constant influx of immigrants from around the world. The then newly christened Board of Health saw the threat of open sewage ditches and thus collected tax revenues to construct a major underground system in which to properly dispose of human waste and rainwater runoff. Being situated on an island, it was all too convenient to have the waste flow dumped into the rivers and harbor.

After a few minutes, Ravenwood and Marya came to a central juncture that joined two tunnels and once again stopped to survey the area. Ravenwood could hear cascading water coming from the tunnel to their left. It seemed to curve slightly and then he smelled the pungent odor of brine. They had to be approaching the river.

He heard footsteps moving away in that very direction. He signaled Marya and began increasing his pace. If that was Baron Savigne ahead of them, Ravenwood guessed he was in for a surprise. Marya kept up with him, being careful not to slip as she too was weary of the dirty water.

When they came around the bend in the tunnel, the blade's knife illuminated Baron Henri Savigne standing at the edge of a twenty-foot precipice that dropped into a collecting pool alongside of a submerged iron grating beyond which extended a four foot pipe that jutted out over the river.

The baron spun around and without warning threw himself forward. He came off his feet and actually flew the ten-foot distance between them. Caught unprepared, Ravenwood was knocked backwards off his feet. In the process Marya was pushed into the wall banging her forehead. She collapsed in a swoon.

Savigne had landed atop the Stepson of Mystery and was now reaching for his throat with his hands while he opened his mouth to reveal his yellowish, extended fangs.

"Chase after me will you?" he spit out, drool falling from his open mouth. "I will make you suffer for such impudence."

Ravenwood, still dazed by the assault, raised his head out of the foul water just as the vampire lord's hands took hold of his neck and began to squeeze. He started to bring his hands up and realized the right still held Marya's butcher blade. Just as Savigne's head came down towards his face, Ravenwood swung out with the knife. The edge sliced across the vampire's open mouth from side to side, tearing the flesh in the process.

Savigne screamed and fell back on his legs as Ravenwood tried to sit up. Filled with rage, the vampire's left hand struck out and grabbing the blade tore it out of Ravenwood's hand and tossed it away.

"BASTARD!!!" he roared. "Now I will suck every drop of blood from your worthless body."

Baron Savigne once again pressed down on the struggling human, pushing down the struggling Ravenwood's head, shoving it back into the water with one hand while exposing his jugular. For Ravenwood only one thought remained; if this was to be his end he would not die easily. He continued to bat away at the ancient fiend as it began to lower its fangs into his neck.

But Savigne never finished his attack for at that very moment Marya rose up behind him holding her thick knife in both hands and drove it in to the vampire's back to the hilt. Again Savigne knew pain and reacted like the animal he was. He twisted about and backhanded Marya across the face propelling her back toward the lip of the tunnel's end.

He tried to reach behind to take hold of the offending blade but couldn't reach it no matter how hard he tried.

Jumping to his feet and ignoring Ravenwood completely, the French vampire pushed himself towards the semi-conscious woman.

"You bitch! All of this was your fault! You couldn't just accept your fate. You had to run and bring about this folly." As he drew closer, Savigne's mindless rage filled his thoughts with the indignities he had been made to suffer because of Marya Dracula. "As if you could ever hope to win out. Foolish, stupid bitch!"

Standing over her, Baron Savigne reached down, grabbed a handful of Marya's hair and pulled her head up roughly. She moaned in pain.

"Time to die."

"NOOOOO!" Ravenwood came out of the darkness behind Savigne and tackled him causing him to let go of Marya and together they fell over the edge.

Into the catch pool they plunged all the way to its cement bottom only three feet deep.

Ravenwood lost his breath under the water but kept his hold on the vampire. Now Savigne was thrashing and somehow manage to find his feet so that he erupted out of the salty water in pure panic.

Salt! Ravenwood broke the surface and gasped for air. Of course, the Hudson was an estuary and it flowed both ways; fresh water from the north, salt water from the south. And it was this element that was consuming Baron Savigne. Just as the table salt had destroyed the vampire back in the diner the previous evening, so the Atlantic brine was having the same affect on the baron. Crazily he tried to pull at the iron grading facing the exit pipe as to climb out of the deadly water but Ravenwood wouldn't let him.

With what strength he had left, he reached up and pulled the vampire back into the pool and then fell over him. It was like riding a slippery seal as Savigne flopped around in the burning pool, the flesh coming off his body in huge chunks. He managed to push Ravenwood off once but his face was nearly gone. Ravenwood felt him weakening and again pulled him down. There was one final convulsion and then the monster stopped moving. Holding him down, Ravenwood came out of the water and took a gulp of air. There was no more movement under his hands.

Releasing his hold, he watched as what remained of Baron Savigne floated to the surface. Most of the flesh had been burned away and only the skeletal frame was visible under the baron's clothing. Though almost totally exhausted, the Stepson of Mystery reached over and pulled the butcher's knife free and then turning the floating corpse around, held the skull while he cut it off at the neck. Once done, he moved to the iron bars and shoved it through one of the square gaps. It was washed away and out the pipe's other end.

"Are you alright?"

Ravenwood turned from the grating and looked up at Marya, kneeling near the tunnel's edge. Her face was bloodied and there were a few bruises he could make out. Luckily his spell on the knife was still active and lit the space.

"I think so."

"Is there a way out of the pool?"

Ravenwood sloshed across the pool to the wall and holding the blade was thankful to see small iron rungs welded into it. "Yes. Hold on."

Slowly, his feet slippery on the rungs, he climbed up to the tunnel floor and there Marya helped him over the lip where they both fell back and sat in silence, wet and cold...and mercifully alive.

Finally she turned to him, wiping a smear of blood off her cheek with her soaked sleeve of her dress and smiled. "Thank you."

Ravenwood looked at her face in the eerie light of the blade, here in this dungeon-like place and thought it was the most beautiful thing he had ever seen.

He touched her bruised cheek and leaned forward to kiss her.

Marya started to pull away only to look into his eyes. One was blue and one was green. Both held only warmth and love.

He leaned in again and their lips touched.

ᴧ

TWO MONTHS LATER –

The wind at the top of the world was always crying as it slipped through the ragged jutting teeth of the Himalayas. It was a mournful howl mostly unheard above five thousand feet where a desolate landscape of white threatened any that dared venture up into its frozen solitude.

Three such fools clung to the side of a mountain pass working their way along a rock ledge as the wind tugged at their burdensome clothing. Cleated boots came down purposefully wary of icy patches that could send the climber spiraling off into space and to a sure death far, far below amidst the gaping chasms.

At the lead, Ravenwood moved with his torso leaning forward, his face all but hidden by a heavy woolen scarf and furred hood. He, like Marya and Jazzy, wore goggles to protect his eyes from the bitter cold. They were tied together by a coarse horsehair rope given to them by the Sherpa guides who had accompanied them to the midpoint in their journey.

Courage, my son, you are almost there. The voice of the Nameless One was still present inside his mind and Ravenwood could not help but marvel at his mentor's mental prowess.

It had been the Nameless One's idea all along after Ravenwood, Marya and Stagg's police detachment had cleaned up the vampire nest at the dockside warehouse. All of them assumed that when Baron Savigne failed to report to the Imperial Vampire Court others would be dispatched to find Marya and her daughter. The undead would never give up. Thus it was paramount that they find a sanctuary where they would be safe from their foes; a place no evil could ever discover or overcome.

That place was the Hidden City where the Nameless One had brought Ravenwood when he was a child and there, with other monks, taught him all manners of oriental philosophies and magics. Thus, when he had put forth the idea, the Stepson of Mystery knew it was the only logical solution.

So had begun their long journey crossing the Pacific by luxury liner and then crossing the vast breadth of China by rail until reaching Nepal and the city of Kathmandu three days ago. Here Ravenwood had hired two Sherpa guides and the final leg of their trek began on a frigid, October day.

To their credit, both Marya and Jazzy had endured the arduous climb with silent strength, though he could see in their faces that they were both physically drained. They plodded along behind him like sleepwalkers following his lead unwaveringly. When the path they were on entered into a hidden cave in the mountain, all of them were relieved to be out of the brutal wind.

"How are you both doing?" Ravenwood leaned back against the cave's interior wall and pulled the stiff scarf from his face.

Marya did the same before replying. "Please, tell me we don't have much further to go." He could see the hint of doubt in her green eyes and it bothered him that they would soon be parting company. The intimacy they had shared these past week had been precious to both of them.

"The Nameless One is still in contact with me." He pointed a gloved hand to his head. "He says we are almost there and he's right. Though it's been ten years since I was here."

"Tell me they have hot food there?' Jazzy begged. She was aware of the change in the relationship between her mother and Ravenwood and mischievously teased Marya whenever he wasn't present.

My son, do not stop. You must keep moving.

"That and much, much more," he said and then pushed away from the wall. "Let's go."

He led them through the cave, which opened to another chasm across which was a small wooden bridge. On the other side was another cave.

Without stopping, Ravenwood crossed the snow-covered span and entered the second cave. He continued to move through the spacious opening until finally the air about them began to feel warm. Ten minutes later it was hot as they reached a huge opening and found themselves looking down at one of the most unique vistas in the entire world.

There stretched out below them was a long valley split by a winding river. There were green hills and forest to either side and they could make out the thatched roofs of small villages.

"Oh, my God," Marya removed her scarf and hood. Then she pulled off her goggles. The others did the same. "Is this place real or are we hallucinating?"

"Oh, it's very real, I assure." Ravenwood smiled happily. Then he pointed to the left where a wide dirt road from the valley went up to a fantastic complex of snow-white buildings. "That's the monastery, where you'll be staying. It was my home once."

Marya and Jazzy held hands and looked down on the white buildings, each surrounded by lush, colorful gardens.

"It's like the Garden of Eden," Jazzy suggested. "Look, someone is coming!"

A bald headed monk in a brown robe and wearing sandals was riding up a winding path to them on the back of a burro. When he reached them, he slid off his mount and greeted them.

"We've been expecting you, Ravenwood. It is good to see you again." He turned and smiled at Marya and Jazzy. "I am Brother Thaddeus. Welcome to Shangri-La."

THE END

YOU *CAN* GO HOME AGAIN

ifteen years ago I wrote a 108 page graphic novel script called "The Daughter of Dracula." In it, Marya Dracula, the only surviving heir of the infamous vampire, Count Dracula, met a young German lad named Manfred von Richthofen just prior to the start of World War One. She at that time was a 500 year old vampire and became infatuated with the young man; enough to keep tabs on him when the war broke out. Of course von Richthofen, a real historical figure, was to go on to become the most deadly German aviation ace of them all nicknamed the Red Baron.

Marya travels to Berlin at the height of his fame and seduces him thus beginning a torrid love affair that last until von Richthofen is actually shot down and killed. Marya is enraged by his death and declares war against the allied pilots...until she discovers she is actually pregnant with Manfred's child; that pregnancy ends her curse and she is human once again; no longer a vampire. The book closes with Marya leaving Transylvania behind, very much pregnant and looking forward to starting her new, fully human life again with her child.

Nine years ago artist Rob Davis read that script and decided he wanted to bring it to visual life. It would take him two years to complete the project. Thus seven years ago we self-published "The Daughter of Dracula" via Rob's own imprint, Redbud Studio and it has gone on to much critical acclaim. We continue to sell it at Amazon and personally at our convention appearancse and its audience continues to grow. People are surprised by the book's positive ending and the honest romance at the core of the tale. Which pleases Rob and me greatly.

Anyway, up until a few months ago I thought Marya's story was finished. Although as her creator, there was always that part of me that wondered what had happened to her after the end of the graphic novel. Did she have the baby? Was it a boy or a girl? Where did they go to live out their lives? Those questions have buzzed around in my noggin for the past seven years. Then out of the blue, writer Josh Reynolds suggested we do an anthology starring occult detectives. Just like that we had Joel Jenkins and Jim Beard on board. Each of these three talented writers had their own heroes, which they had invented; whereas we needed one more tale to fill the book. Which was when I got the idea of writing a Ravenwood – Stepson of Mystery adventure. Airship 27 had already done two anthologies with the hero and I was particularly eager to try my own hand at writing him.

But what would I write? And then, as so often happens, the muse began talking to me. What if Marya Dracula came to New York City with her child and crossed paths with Ravenwood? But why? Because they were being chased by vampires....and then just like a row of dominoes falling one atop the other, the plot to "Jazzy," exploded full blown in my imagination and there she was…Marya and Manfred's child, now a beautiful, spunky teenage girl. From that point on I couldn't write this story fast enough. I pray you enjoyed it and if you haven't read "Daughter of Dracula," will go out and pick up a copy. Whereas if you are a dedicated fan of that graphic novel, I hope you liked seeing Marya again and meeting Jazemara Dracula.

For me, it was very much like coming home again.

RON FORTIER - A veteran comic book creator, he's best known for writing the Green Hornet and Terminator:Burning Earth, with Alex Ross, for Now Comics back in the 90s. Today, he keeps busy writing and editing new pulp anthologies and novels via his Airship 27 Productions (http://robmdavis.com/Airship27Hangar/airship27hangar.html). He won the Pulp Factory Award for Best Pulp Short Story of 2011 for "Vengeance Is Mine" which appeared in *The Avenge – Justice Inc.* from Moonstone Books and again in 2012 for "The Ghoul," which appeared in *Monster Aces*.

He continues to write his own graphic novels and series, such as Mr. Jigsaw Man of a Thousands Parts via Redbud Studio. (http://www.robmdavis.com/RedbudStudio/index.html)

You can keep updated with his latest projects by visiting his personal website at: (www.airship27.com)

The Return of
RAVENWOOD

He is an orphan raised by a Tibetan mystic known only as *Nameless One* and taught Eastern magics from the dawn of time. As an Occult Detective he has no equal and is called upon by the authorities when they are challenged by super-natural mysteries. One of the more obscure pulp characters, *Ravenwood – The Stepson of Mystery* appeared as a back-up feature in the pages of *Secret Agent X* magazine. There were only five Ravenwood stories ever written, all by his creator, the prolific pulp veteran, Frederick C. Davis.

Now he returns in a brand new series of weird adventures, beginning with this volume in which he combats *Sun Koh*, a lost prince of Atlantis, battles with monstrous Yetis in Manhattan and deals with murderous ghosts and zombie assassins.

New pulp storytellers Frank Schildiner, B.C. Bell, Bill Gladman and Bobby Nash offer up a quartet of fast paced, bizarre thrillers that rekindle the excitement and wonder that were the pulps.

With a stunning cover by Bryan Fowler and dramatic interior illustrations by Charles Fetherolf, *Ravenwood – Stepson of Mystery* was designed by Rob Davis and edited by Ron Fortier. Once again Airship 27 Productions presents pulp fans with another quality pulp reading experience like no other on the market today.

Daughter of Dracula

During World War One, Marya Dracula, the five hundred year old daughter of Count Dracula, becomes infatuated with Manfred von Richthofen, the famous flying ace known as the Red Baron. She seduces him and they have a torrid love affair against the background of war. But when he uncovers her dark secret and chooses to become one of the undead like her, it sets into motion a terrible chain of events neither is prepared for. Horror and eroticism mix to create a truly unique, adult melodrama.